Roxana Nastase

Team Building with a Twist

Cozy Mystery

Scarlet Leaf

2019

Table of Contents

To Sebastian Stan, a man with a golden heart, although he would like that we believed differently
I am happy to have been given the chance to know you

Acknowledgements

I would like to thank my managers for their exceptional understanding and help throughout this creative process: *Ahmed Ferchichi*, *Adrian Hobjila* and *Taoufik Rai*.

I can only do so alphabetically as they have all been amazing this past month and deserve equally my utmost gratitude.

Without you, this book would not exist today.

Thank you.

CHAPTER ONE

He looked like an unkempt bed, rugged and mussed—perfect advertising for an orgy. One hand on the mouse, eyes slightly glassed, Gabriel didn't move a muscle, afraid that his head would split in two, despite the hangover fog turning his brain to mush.

All of a sudden, a string of blue swearing filled the room and drowned the tapping of fingers on the keyboards. Several heads popped up, and a few chortles joined in the fray.

Gabriel cringed, and the pulse in his temples went up a notch. Still, he didn't blink or look up, not even when the guffaws grew louder in the wake of the most inventive cusswords ever voiced on the floor.

A braver sunray hit the right angle, pouring more light through the blinds behind. Dust motes flew in the air, and Gabriel's eyes narrowed to slits. Nausea grabbed his stomach in a powerful fist and squeezed. He gulped, trying to process the noise.

He knew that he should have intervened. Andy had already crossed the line, and big time. However, opening his mouth felt like too much of an effort. Gabriel's thoughts still rolled around the previous night's debacle. He had simply made an ass of himself.

Exhaustion flirted with his eyelids, but then a mean stubborn streak in his genetic code forbade him to surrender to it.

Sick of the caterwauling on the floor, Gabriel looked up and snarled, "Cut it out, Andy. Do your job and suck it up."

"Come on, Gabriel, you should come and see what this sorry ass is saying here," Andy retorted plaintively, stroking his thick dark goatee.

Gabriel almost gave in. He did have a soft spot for the massive guy, who topped up at 5.9 feet and weighed about 240 pounds. However, he smothered his impulse when another round of chortles rolled over the floor. One of the guys had even started tapping his hands on the top of his desk, while his feet kept the rhythm on the floor.

"That's enough of that," Gabriel ordered in a stern tone of voice. "I see three chats waiting in the queue," his voice cut them off, when he glanced at the screen hanging over his head. "Why not take those instead of receding to kindergarten?"

"Come on, man," Alex intervened. "It's not like we aren't working here, you know," he pointed out, a bite of anger stealing into his voice.

"It doesn't look like that from where I stand," Gabriel bit back. "I've got things to do. Do your job, and stop fooling around. When the queue shows zero, do whatever you want," he thundered, and a sharp pain shot between his temples.

Gabriel blocked out his people's smirks and frustrated whispers and went back to staring at the graph on his computer screen. The chart still reigned there in all its glory, mocking Gabriel's efforts to earn an honest pay that morning.

He took another look at it. Nope, no matter the angle, he still couldn't make heads or tails out of it.

It seemed more entertaining to listen to Andy's creative cussing than trying to decipher that graph, so Gabriel scowled, ready to stick his tongue out at it.

As he had always counted Andy among the good guys, Gabriel regretted that he had had to bring the law down on him. The young man might have bitched a lot, but he got the work done in the end.

The graph still danced before Gabriel's eyes, taunting him, so he decided to change his focus for a moment and take an aspirin or two.

Exasperated, he rummaged through his drawer cabinet. Finding the bottle of aspirin, he swallowed two in short order, a sulk turning the corners of his mouth down.

He hated the taste of drugs. It lingered on his tongue long after he had washed it down his throat.

Gabriel leaned back in his chair, slowly breathed in and out, waiting for the oblivion to hit. His tension headache had just staved off a little when another litany of swearing blew out.

Gabriel knew that soon enough, he would have to step in, given Andy's tone of voice. Else, Andy would punch the top of the desk. The guy was fired up big time.

Andy had been working with their team for almost a year. His actions were nothing if not predictable, and most of the time, he expressed his feelings with flair.

His baritone voice would carry all over the floor, and that often brought complaints from the voice department.

That didn't bother Gabriel. His own team plagued him with enough worries, so he didn't have any strength left to think about others.

It was their problem not his if they couldn't deal with the noise. The spewing of nasty words was something common on the floor. It came with the territory.

Those who thought that working on chat was easy-peasy had no idea what they were talking about. Sometimes it was nerve-wracking work, and people needed to express themselves in one way or another. Gabriel didn't mind it unless he went through a hangover.

The guy doing the cursing right then wasn't the only source of filthy words on the floor. Even Gabriel went at it sometimes, and with enthusiasm.

Most of the time, expletives would come from all over the floor, and not always in the baritone voice of a man. Such invectives sometimes flew off soft lips, the suave, delicate voices in stark contrast with the crude sounds uttered under pressure.

To Gabriel's dismay, Andy's swearing didn't stop soon enough to satisfy him.

"Andy," he barked. "I said cut it out," he shouted, fire in his voice.

Andy's sweet words changed their destination, but Gabriel turned a deaf ear, pretending he didn't listen to him.

"Who the hell, does he think he is?" Andy growled, his fingers tapping furiously on his keyboard. It wasn't as if he couldn't write and have a conversation with his neighbor, Dan, at the same time.

"Probably, he thinks he is the boss," Dan replied dryly, and Anna, who sat next to him, bumped him over the shoulder with an enthusiastic thump.

"You fiend," she giggled, brushing her hair behind her ears and pulling her dress lower off her shoulders to give everyone a better view.

Gabriel rolled his eyes, although a sparkle of pity gleamed inside him. Anna had been advertising her wares for some time now, and Gabriel was sick and tired of it. He didn't have the heart to ask her to stop it, but she did put his teeth on edge with the display of her bony, pimple-covered shoulders.

With a shake of his head, Gabriel forgot about her and glanced toward Andy, realizing he shouldn't allow the guy's words to slide. However, after a couple of seconds, he reconsidered his thoughts with a shrug. His head was killing him, and he didn't need any more grief.

Lately, Gabriel had been drinking heavily although the booze didn't help him sleep any better. His alcohol-fueled nights had merely hatched vivid and noise-drowned nightmares, which haunted him even in the daytime.

"Gabriel, I've been taking chats for an hour and a half without break now, and there are others who aren't doing anything," an angry voice sneaked into his thoughts.

Gabriel's eyes turned to the side, where a heavyset young man had braced his elbows on top of his desk.

"Remind me what are we paying you for?" Gabriel asked through his teeth.

A red mist crept over the guy's face and neck, and his throat tried to swallow down.

"I know what I'm paid for," he started, but Gabriel didn't allow him to continue.

"Then continue doing your job, Al, and stop looking over other people's shoulder," he said in a hard tone of voice to conclude the conversation.

"I am doing my damn job," Al growled. "But why should I work my ass off for a measly pay when others have it for a lark?"

"Really, Al? Only for a lark?" Gabriel countered, narrowing his eyes to slits.

"Yeah, like your girlfriend there," Al pointed his chin toward a dark-haired girl, who was leaning in her chair, her legs tucked beneath her while browsing through a catalogue.

Gabriel glanced at the woman and gnashed his teeth, guilt gnawing at him. Nevertheless, he didn't back down.

"As I said before, you shouldn't be checking what others are doing. If you'd been as busy as you claim you were, you wouldn't have had any time for that," he pointed out.

"Look here," Al smacked his fist on the top of the desk, losing his temper.

"No, you look here," Gabriel pierced him with a laser-like gaze. "If you're tired, take a damn break and leave me the heck alone. I have work to do. I'll take care of the others later."

Al chewed his lower lip for a few seconds, then nodded and straightened up. He turned to go back to his desk but couldn't refrain from spitting through his teeth, "Jerk."

Gabriel's first impulse was to bite back and take him to task. He opened his mouth for a stiff reprimand, but then changed his mind and shrugged.

The man was right. Some people cashed their paycheck without doing the work. Gabriel could have gotten into the face of some of them, but not all of them. With a sigh, he returned to his work.

A heavy headset covered his ears, yet all the noises in the room mingled in a cacophony that threatened to insinuate into his thoughts. That constant racket should have shuttered the man's hard-acquired peace, but that didn't bother Gabriel. A veteran of the floor, he had almost become immune to the surrounding clamor and seldom lost his focus.

"Need to talk to you," a heavy hand fell on Gabriel's shoulder, and the suddenness of the unexpected gesture, as well as the harshness of the tone, almost startled him.

CHAPTER TWO

Gabriel subdued his reactions with a steely hand. His boss's words might have sounded like an invitation, but the tone of the man's voice had changed that request into an order.

Gabriel took his eyes off his computer screen lazily, and not only because he was playing a role. Sudden moves made him dizzy, and he didn't feel like losing his consciousness and hitting the floor in a dead faint at his boss's feet.

He looked up, putting on a poker face, so that his thoughts wouldn't reflect on his features. It was no one else's business that he felt depleted, or that the sand under his eyelids grated on his nerves.

His long limbs and fingers didn't betray his inner struggle. He ordered his body to relax and breathed out soundlessly, refusing to allow the intruder to perceive his inner tension.

Now that his head had popped up, a few spikes in his hair slashed the air with a faint whoosh. His amber eyes set earnestly on his boss's face, and a second later, Gabriel's boyish smile hit the bull's-eye target.

Adam, his hand still firmly squeezing Gabriel's shoulder, lifted his left eyebrow. He had known Gabriel for a while, but the guy still surprised him. Not many people could do that.

Gabriel felt awkward under the light pressure of his boss's touch. He wished that Adam would take his hand away, and soon. Gabriel enjoyed less human contact than that. Yet, his lips curved, a hint of irony lingering in the left corner of his mouth.

He trusted that deceptively sincere smile, tainted with a tinge of mischief. It had become one of his best weapons and helped him to cover his inherent shyness. After all, he had rehearsed it in front of the mirror for days on end. That grin had taken down enemies, but mostly had pushed his diffidence away.

Now, the new Gabriel he had painstakingly created came through the tawny, hair-blown, self-confident young man he had become. No one knew of his fears. Most of the time, he hid them even from himself.

"Let's have a cigarette," Adam, Gabriel's manager said, searching the younger man's face with curiosity. Gabriel seemed somewhat remote and not completely there.

"I was thinking about quitting smoking," Gabriel grumbled, standing up with a slothful move, careful not to teeter on his shaky legs, showing to all and sundry how pitiful he felt.

Gabriel had a fair idea what the talk with Adam would involve, and he wasn't in the right frame of mind to face his manager right then. Lately, his people had started to come late for their shift, or hadn't bothered to come at all.

Summer lulled everyone. No one really cared about anything other than a trip to the sea or the mountains. Any work ethic that had existed before almost vanished, and it hadn't been too much to begin with.

Gabriel had tried to make his people think beyond the moment and failed. He hadn't missed their smirks during the last briefs and could have reiterated their conversations after those meetings in detail.

"And have you quit already?" Adam asked, his penetrating black eyes fixed on Gabriel's face.

'*By God, he's got such an uncanny skill not to blink when he stares at someone,*' Gabriel thought.

"No, not really," Gabriel grumbled. "You know how it is. Something or another comes up all the time. It makes it harder to stop smoking," Gabriel said with a rueful smirk on his lips.

"Well, either way, we still have to talk," Adam shrugged and turned toward the door overlooking the terrace. "I'll have a cigarette if you don't want one, and you can keep me company," the man threw over his shoulder.

Adam's steely voice didn't promise anything good, and a cold shiver ran along Gabriel's spine. Caught in a maze of personal misery, Gabriel didn't really feel able to deal with anything at that moment, but he knew that he didn't have a choice. Deep down, he suspected that either he didn't have anything more to give to that job, or he needed a change of scenery.

However, paying the rent held him back. He was stuck in that place in the meanwhile and had to answer to Adam.

"I'll smoke a cigarette with you," he replied and started rummaging through his drawer cabinet looking for one. He hadn't rolled any more cigarettes lately with the hope that it would make quitting smoking easier.

Adam strode toward the door of the terrace without waiting for him. Gabriel smirked inwardly, covertly following his boss's progress from the corner of his eye.

He found a couple of cigarettes forgotten in one of the drawers and straightened, ready to go out as well. A silky voice called his name, dripping longing and hatred into his blood.

Gabriel breathed deeply and turned to Mia, the almond-eyed, dark fairy, who had played him with sweetness and shyness, concealing her mercenary soul until she got what she wanted.

Sometimes, he reviled the woman with a blinding passion. Most of the time, he tried hard to forget about her presence on the floor. He didn't need a sexual harassment law suit so he kept his distance and his mouth shut.

Whenever his eyes fell on her, he reflected that men were indeed stupid. Now, he looked at her and sighed inwardly. '*I seem to be getting the-idiot-of-the-year prize,*' he mused.

"I can't help you now," he replied to Mia in a flat tone of voice. "I have a meeting. Go talk to Andy or Alex, if you need help," he said and went out the door.

Gabriel strode onto the terrace with ostensibly unbridled energy, and his eyes fell on his manager.

Adam, blind and deaf to the loud traffic noises coming from down in the street, lounged in a lawn chair, deep in his thoughts. At the sound of the door opening, his eyes zeroed in on Gabriel, a faint grin tucked in the corner of his mouth.

Gabriel never walked or strolled when he could storm, and he did that most of the time. The young man didn't seem capable to rein very well the geyser of energy residing in his body. His distance-eating stride went well hand in hand with his way of talking loudly and fast, to better cover anyone else's opinions.

Adam had often wondered if that behavior proved either Gabriel's selfishness or insecurity. Anyway, he liked the man enough even though he seemed an enigma sometimes.

Although well shy of the 6 feet mark – just 5.7 feet, always the bane of his existence in a world where movies and books pushed for tall and well-built males, Gabriel's lanky silhouette sported long limbs, vibrating with unharnessed vitality, strong hands, a tawny mop of a head, and amber eyes framed with long and thick, tawny lashes.

Adam's unnerving gaze measured the younger man, and with an imperceptible shudder, Gabriel sensed that he had been carved and analyzed to the core in a matter of seconds. That annoyed him. He flexed his fingers around his lighter, reflecting that his manager might have observed much more than Gabriel had intended to let him see.

Adam always disconcerted with his piercing glances and his resolute eyes. He had the power to make Gabriel lose some of his so hard-acquired self-assured polish, and Gabriel loathed that.

Not only did Adam's dark clever eyes make Gabriel circumspect around him, but also the ruthlessness hidden behind the jovial façade Adam showed to the world. A master in mystification, Gabriel easily spotted another one when he faced him.

He didn't entertain any illusions about his boss. When someone mentioned Adam's compassionate and kind nature within earshot of him, Gabriel barely hid his amusement. Adam wouldn't avoid stepping on people if it could serve his purpose.

Adam watched Gabriel for a few more seconds and then inquired, "Another late night?"

Gabriel shrugged and replied lightly, "No later than others."

Then, he sprawled on the lawn chair across from Adam. He busied himself, arranging his cigarettes and lighter on the lawn table before him.

Gabriel breathed in the hot summer air, spoiled with exhaust, and welcomed the weak breeze, which cooled his feverish skin.

His eyes darted discreetly around to see if there was anyone else present on the terrace. He didn't like witnesses when he was being dressed down. Nonetheless, he knew that someone always came out for a cigarette or a breather so he didn't hope for too much.

Silence stretched for a minute or two, getting on Gabriel's nerves. He had learned the basics about handling people and the best tactics to employ, so he knew to keep silent and wait for Adam to speak first. However, the busy traffic in the street didn't make the quietness on the terrace less awkward, and his tension went slightly up.

"Got anything on your mind?" Gabriel slipped and inquired, berating himself a second later because he had just broken his golden rule.

"As a matter of fact... yes," Adam replied.

Gabriel clamped his teeth at Adam's hard tone. Adam's easy-going façade had disappeared, and the hard glint in his eyes called to attention now.

Gabriel lit one of the cigarettes and shoved the lighter in his pants pocket, taking his sweet time. He still needed to gather his scattered thoughts if he wanted to get out of this impromptu meeting with his pride intact.

Finishing with the smoking rituals, he leaned back in his lawn chair. He rolled his shoulders imperceptibly, trying to ease the tension in the knotted muscles at the back of his neck. His fingers itched to rub them, but he didn't dare to do it.

The drumming in his temples had intensified once more, the aspirins all but forgotten, and the dryness of his mouth prompted his tongue to brush over his upper teeth. Unconsciously, he ruffled his hair with nervous fingers and then looked up at Adam, a small self-deprecating grin in the corner of his mouth.

"I think I know what it is you want to talk about," Gabriel said very matter-of-factly.

He kept his eyes on Adam's stern features, while drawing smoke into his lungs. From the corner of his eye, he spied a magpie, vaulting in a high arch across the street, the sudden move speaking of freedom, something he secretly craved.

Freedom was a relative term, he reflected, inhaling the smoke. Right then it meant that he could go home, pull the blinds and burrow between the sheets.

"I imagine you do," Adam replied in a dry tone of voice, drawing Gabriel's attention back to him. "It's no secret that the chat department is rapidly drowning in issues," Adam started his lecture. "And most of the problems come from your team, not Lara's," Adam pointed out.

He fastened his eyes on Gabriel's face and braced his left ankle on his knee, the first gesture hinting that he might be on the brink of losing his temper.

Gabriel didn't mind it when people lost their cool. He could deal with that. Adam's cold and steely attitude was something else.

"Yes, we've had several breaches of internal regulation," Gabriel started to explain but didn't get further.

Adam interrupted him with an impatient wave of his hand, even though his voice remained steady and didn't betray any of his irritation.

"It's not merely about internal regulation violations, Gabriel, although those are numerous enough to make people talk," he stressed out.

His eyes pierced the younger man with their black sparkle.

"I've also noticed a serious drop in quality and performance, and not only me. The powers that be have made a note of that too."

Gabriel didn't reply, as he couldn't argue with that. He had already felt the results of his people's poor work. His bonus had dropped by thirty percent, and he could have used that money.

"And I should also mention the tension thriving on the floor," Adam continued.

The wrinkles around his eyes deepened, and his lips thinned. "That tension... Not so good for productivity. Huh? What do you think?"

Gabriel winced under the chill of Adam's words. He couldn't dispute them, though.

The atmosphere in the department had been getting edgier for a few months already, and even his plans of having the team order food together or going out now and then hadn't worked.

"I can't put my finger on it, but I feel that you factor in this tense situation, as well," Adam said, his voice full of disbelief.

He did know Gabriel and always admired his easiness in managing his people.

"And that does seem weird. I have always believed that you were well liked and respected by your team, but now...," Adam shook his head in confusion.

"I understand what you're saying," Gabriel replied quietly, a slight edge in his voice. He had been aware that his presence fed the stress on the floor.

He had changed somehow lately. He had begun growing clumsy in managing his people, and his moods had become unpredictable. He gave a passing thought to his drinking binges, but he wasn't ready to accept them as the root of that change.

"Are you sure you understand?" Adam asked him with clipped words, and the tone of his voice whiplashed through Gabriel.

The two men looked at one another for a few moments. Adam's stance displayed resolution. Gabriel just focused on breathing.

Two guys from the voice department came out on the terrace laughing. Both Adam and Gabriel turned their heads toward them, and the guys halted, anxiety etched on their faces.

"We'll just go to the other side," the taller one said, pointing to the other corner of the terrace.

They strode in that direction with hurried steps, as far as possible from the two of them. They had stopped laughing and didn't exchange a word.

Adam waited for a few moments until the guys' steps faded, then he continued.

"That girl, Mia, the one you brought on the project from downstairs, although I said that you shouldn't, you remember." Adam punctuated his words with a sharp wave of his hand.

Gabriel just waited for the other shoe to drop, and a powerful fist squeezed his heart.

"She's not doing anything," Adam concluded in a deadpan tone of voice.

"I've noticed," Gabriel practically growled. "Should I mention that I asked to have her in Lara's team from the beginning?" he replied smartly.

He thought that shifting the blame would do him some good.

"I didn't ask to have her in my team, and I had solid reasons for that. Lara should have kept her," he pointed out, crossing his ankles in a diffident gesture. "I think that Lara should be concerned of Mia's performance, as well."

Gabriel never found out what had happened between Mia and Lara, but two days after Mia started working in their department, Lara announced him that she would move Mia to his team. That did slap his expectations down and turned his days into a living nightmare.

Mia's stubbornness rivaled a mule's. She didn't give a fig about what she was supposed to do or about receiving feedback either. She just sailed away after each discussion, indifferent to Gabriel's efforts to whip her into shape.

The woman seemed interested in flaunting her generous silhouette to him, and every other male in sight. Her only purpose was to make them drool. As one of the guys said, Mia was nothing else but a big tease.

More often than not, she made herself scarce from her desk when she should have been working, so the others bitched because she got the same pay without pulling her weight.

Besides, Mia loved to hurt and belittle everyone, and Gabriel feared that soon he would have an open revolt on his hands.

Most of his recent headaches sprung from sleepless nights, filled with half-assed plans and an impotent search for a solution.

He had tried to talk it out with Mia, but she had cut it short. She had even hinted at filing a sexual harassment complaint with the HR, although she didn't have grounds for that as Gabriel had stepped back and hadn't hinted at any relationship with her once she became his subordinate.

He didn't fear that he would be found guilty if an investigation ensued. However, that newly acquired fame would stop his advancement in the company. People always believed the worst.

"Not really," Adam pierced Gabriel with a sharp glance. "It's not Lara's responsibility. You brought Mia here," he pointed out. "She's in your team. You deal with her."

Gabriel ran his fingers through his hair. He seemed like he wanted to say something but gave up.

"Why did you bring her here? I don't care," Adam shrugged. "I guess she had probably pushed all your buttons to make sure she gets hired. Then, she pushed Lara's, so that she'd become your responsibility. So, take her in hand. It's your job," he reiterated, and his eyes pierced Gabriel with their arctic blue.

For a moment, Gabriel forgot himself and grimaced. He tapped his cigarette, avoiding Adam's gaze.

Damned if he did, damned if he didn't. Taking Mia in hand would have been far from a simple job, and he didn't even know where to begin.

Adam noticed Gabriel's uncertainty and continued, "As I said, I don't care how you do it. Just do it. Got it?"

Gabriel nodded, and Adam pressed his lips in a thin line. He doubted that Gabriel would do anything about Mia and knew that he would have to step in and do Gabriel's job. He didn't dislike anything more than getting involved in such things.

"Other than Mia," Adam said, leaning back in his lawn chair, "there are others, for instance, Anna."

"What about Anna?" Gabriel asked, and his eyes widened in surprise. He had never wasted too many thoughts on Anna. Her work didn't hit the top, but it was all right and passed the quality requirements.

"Come on, you can't tell me that you haven't noticed the manner she dresses and how she acts," Adam cocked his head, staring at Gabriel with disbelief.

Gabriel shrugged Adam's words as inconsequential and waived his hand. "That's just her way, Adam. And she's not the only one in the company who's doing that, after all."

"Maybe she's not," Adam conceded, "but she's the only one wearing those skimpy dresses and acting like a little tramp just to make you look her way," he pointed out.

His eyebrows climbed up his forehead while his eyes bored holes into Gabriel, wondering if the man was so blind that he couldn't see what lay underneath the girl's conduct.

'Even a blind man would see through her behavior,' Adam thought with sarcasm.

"Are you serious?" Gabriel burst into laughter. "I think you're wrong, Adam. You're just imagining things," he shook his head, refusing to believe Adam's assessment.

Anna's dresses and her femme fatale attitude had already become a common occurrence. She came through a bit slutty, but that was her business as she didn't hurt anyone, and probably, the floor would be less entertaining without her presence and usual demeanor.

"Think again," Adam replied sharply. "She's pining on you, all right, and your lack of attention is driving her mad."

Gabriel arched his left eyebrow and grinned, thinking that Adam was joking.

"All right, you won't buy it. Let's touch on other aspects. Her performance dropped almost to fifty percent. Besides, her conduct upsets the other women on the floor and drives some of the guys crazy. Don't tell me that you haven't noticed that either," Adam asked in a hard, sarcastic voice.

Wide-eyed, Gabriel had to concede that he hadn't noticed anything. But then, he hadn't really been present on the floor either, even if his body was.

"Then, there's Andy. I know the guys get frustrated sometimes and need to vent. I get that. But not all the damn time," Adam threw his hands in the air with exasperation.

"I know he might be a bit... obnoxious," Gabriel chose to say. "However, he does his job."

"I can't even read a report when he is on the floor," Adam countered. "I understand jack. And he is just an example. I am sick and tired of hearing that swearing all the time. Plus, I am not the only one."

"I get it. I will talk to them to tone it down to a minimum. Is it all right?" Gabriel asked, willing to end that conversation soon.

He had never been in the position of being whipped into shape, and he loathed it.

"I'm afraid that it won't be enough," Adam shook his head, stirring Gabriel's anxiety a notch. "There are lots of other problems."

"What do you have in mind?" Gabriel asked.

"You need to build the team up from zero again," Adam replied, his words shaking Gabriel's world.

"I know that you have a few new guys, but in reality, the others are at the root of all the issues. Of course, soon, the new hires will learn to emulate the old ones, and that isn't something you'd want. Take my word for it."

"All right, I will think about it," Gabriel said and braced his palms onto the armrests of his chair, ready to push himself up. The impromptu meeting had jaded him more than he thought.

When his eyes fell on the two guys coming back from the other side of the terrace, he ground his teeth.

"I have already thought about it," Adam stopped Gabriel's movement with his hard reply.

First, he waited for the two men to get inside first, and then he continued.

"I will send you the memo," he turned to Gabriel afterward. "I outlined the budget you can count on and jotted down a few ideas for you. You have to build around that. I want to see everything in place in maximum three weeks," he demanded in a tone of voice that didn't allow broaching any argument.

"What should be in place?" Gabriel asked with suspicion.

"You will organize a team building action," Adam said.

Gabriel's eyes widened. He wiped his sweaty palms on his jeans, reflecting that that was just the icing on the cake. He shook his head to clear it, but the cloud in his mind hung on.

"A team building action?" he repeated, his eyes bulging somewhat.

"Yes, that's correct," Adam replied succinctly. "I'll be waiting for a detailed plan," he pointed out.

He searched Gabriel's face and understood that the man was in a daze. He sighed inwardly but pushed forward.

"I don't want to hear something as simple as going to play darts or drink beer. I want real team building. The action should take place over the span of three days. Lara's team will hold the fort while you and your people are away. They will get their turn afterward. Now get cracking," Adam stood up and left the terrace without glancing back at Gabriel.

"Team building," Gabriel whispered with dismay in his voice. "With this crazy lot..." he shook his head. "For three damn days... I'm screwed. I knew it."

CHAPTER THREE

It took Gabriel quite a little over two weeks to build around Adam's plan and organize a team building trip in the mountains, and not only because it was a huge undertaking.

He had needed almost two days just to shake off the leftovers of the harshest hangover he had ever experienced.

He was hardly a virgin when it came to soaking his brains in alcohol. He had gone through other drink binges before when he felt sorry for himself because someone would overlook him or another girl would sail out of his life.

Gabriel's eyes still crossed, and his insides flinched and roiled whenever he remembered Adam's ultimatum day. That was what he called it. He knew that Adam had given him one last chance and nothing more.

Gabriel still couldn't get over the shame and anger that Adam's lecture had stirred. The man had pinpointed his shortcomings without mercy.

Gabriel had been busy during those couple of weeks, and not only with the organization of the team building trip, which had been a real pain in the ass by itself. For a while, it had been touch and go. Mostly go, because Adam had made him change the plans several times.

Gabriel had also succeeded in alienating a few other members of his team beside Mia.

The train rolled along the railway, rocking him gently, while Gabriel leaned back in his seat and watched the landscape fly by his window.

He was breathing in and out to release the stress but could hardly hold his pessimism at bay. Everybody avoided him like the plague.

The others ignored him and had already bunched together around a few tables far away from his seat. Gabriel had expected that, and the smirks or angry gazes directed at him didn't surprise him.

He had lost his people's respect, and that hurt. He had had a fairly good hand with people before coming across Mia. But afterward, his brain marinated in vodka, and he couldn't get a straight thought worth a damn.

The light changed with the altitude, and the green of the woods filled the horizon. He hushed the pang of regret in his chest as whispers came from the other side of the car and let his eyes roam over the houses settled on the sweet slope of a hill.

The inside of his mouth felt dry, coated with dust, so he took the bottle of water from the small table before him and swallowed a mouthful. He screwed the lid back on the bottle, thinking that he didn't hold a hope for that trip.

The sudden thought that he didn't care enough to make it work gave him a jolt of awareness. Then he shrugged. Coming Monday, he would probably be out of the company on his ear anyway. Gabriel had known that Mia wasn't joking around with her threats so the outcome didn't surprise him.

His gaze wandered out of the window. A light breeze danced through the leaves, and a few fluffy clouds spotted the blue of the sky. The tower of a church speared upward through the line of thick trees, which secreted a hamlet.

Mia's voice from somewhere in the car sneaked into his thoughts, reminding him that she hadn't wasted any time after their stormy brief. He had been harsh, and she had yelled right back at him. After the briefing, she had asked for a commission and accused him of sexual harassment, as she had promised. It hurt that he hadn't even got to kiss her.

Staring at the river on the right side of the tracks, Gabriel pushed Mia out of his mind with determination. She wasn't the only one who hated his guts, and he didn't want to give her too much importance. He had wasted enough time thinking of her.

Andy's booming laughter filled the carriage, and Gabriel took his eyes off the valley, turning toward the noise, where Andy was holding court farther ahead in the car, enjoying himself.

Now the easy-going Andy pretended not to notice Gabriel when their paths crossed, or simply looked through him as if he had been made of glass.

Andy's attitude ate at Gabriel. He liked Andy, and the two of them had often cruised the night and the clubs together. Not long ago, they had been as thick as thieves.

Still, Andy hadn't liked being told to watch his mouth on the job. He held strong opinions about freedom of speech and got mad once he concluded that Gabriel curtailed his rights.

Andy was a volcano in disguise and didn't know how to take criticism graciously and build on it. He had sworn to retaliate and pay Gabriel back. Gabriel believed him because Andy never forgot or forgave a thing. He would always get even if he perceived that someone wronged him.

Andy stood up and threw something over the back of his seat. Guffaws erupted all around the table, and unintelligible words joined in the chorus of *'gee, thanks, you jerk,'* which prompted Andy to flip them off.

"Knock it out, you clown," Alex snapped at him.

Andy merely shrugged and turned his back at him. Andy respected Alex. Gabriel should have corralled Alex to help him deal with Andy, but any good ideas he might have had got lost among the clutter in his mind.

Anna left the third table they occupied and started toward the end of the carriage, her eyes trained on the floor, her attitude solely for Gabriel's benefit.

He had invited Anna to a one-on-one meeting the week before and touched on the subject of her clothes or lack thereof, and on her habit of painting her face in war colors.

She hadn't been able to face him without scarlet cheeks and quivering lips ever since.

Gabriel remembered that he had thrown his total lack of interest in her into the mix and grimaced. He had even told her that she needed to start living in the real world.

Now, when their eyes met, which didn't happen often, the deep shadows he spied in her eyes troubled him.

He had wanted to say something different during their meeting, but he had forgotten about his long-rehearsed speech by the time he showed her into the conference room.

He hadn't found a way to atone for his words yet. He was thinking about apologizing to her after he tended his resignation, but then, it might be too late. Their friendship wouldn't last.

Gabriel felt sorry that he hadn't shown Anna more sensibility, or George more understanding. He should have treaded water smoother with Andy or with Mara. He felt like drinking an entire bottle of vodka, and he knew that he shouldn't.

Soon though, he changed his mind. After the train pulled into their station, Gabriel announced the team that he had rented two villas right at the edge of the small mountain town, and they had to hike there. They didn't enjoy the idea and started their complaining.

All of Gabriel's decisions over the last few weeks flew out the window. As he herded his motley crew toward the outskirts of the town, his eyes started searching around to find the best place where he could buy and savor a drink. His ears rang and bled with complaints and cusses, while he put one foot in front of the other up the mountain.

CHAPTER FOUR

An owl screeched from somewhere in the forest, and a new spring appeared in Gabriel's step. His second bottle of vodka slid out of his shaking hand, splashing his pants in the process, but he caught it craftily.

"Hmm, I'm not as drunk as I thought," Gabriel chuckled weakly.

At that point, he gazed around. He noticed the shadows around for the first time and had the feeling that the trees closed in on him. Anxiety clawed at his chest, and a shiver touched his back.

The pathway he had chosen earlier that night skirted around bunches of trees, mostly clustered in the dark. He looked up and stared at the sliver of the moon, partly hidden in the clouds, and shuddered unconsciously.

Gabriel had gazed at the stars for a while, lying down in the glade he had picked as his stopping point a few hours earlier. He had spent most of the evening and night there, downing vodka and smoking himself into a stupor. He had pushed all thoughts at the back of his mind and enjoyed just being.

Now his head ached, and a tickle scratched his throat. However, he forgot about all of that when something shuffled through the leaves and the twigs littering the forest floor.

Gabriel shivered and scrubbed his face with his free hand. Something or someone moved in the dark, and he didn't have the urge to find out what.

The sharp sensation of being watched made him turn around abruptly. His palms sweltered, and a trickle of sweat ran under his tee along his spine.

Something or someone was stalking him, and he didn't need to get acquainted with his stalker.

After a last long gaze behind, he started swiftly down the pathway, in spite of his wobbling feet. The alcohol might have mushed his brain and impaired his footing, but his self-preservation instinct had kicked in. Going down seemed faster than climbing up, even if his eyes darted here and there.

A prey framed in a hunter's telescopic sight, he skimmed over the trees and bushes around. It was so quiet that the slightest sound startled him, and the forest was full of muffled noises and creaks. Behind him, the mountains lay in their splendor, scaring him shitless.

Gritting his teeth, he thought that he would have preferred the smelly and annoying city traffic right then.

It took him another twenty minutes to get back to the villas. By then, he had been gulping for air, and not only because of the effort.

A city boy, he wasn't comfortable either with the eerie silence surrounding him, or the sporadic sounds of the forest, which terrified him. Someone was walking the night all right. Terror had ants crawling all over his spine, filling him with shame.

Gabriel's feet hurt, and his muscles screamed, protesting the long march down the slope of the mountain at a neck-breaking speed. His body lacked stamina, and that wasn't surprising. He had forgotten about going to the gym for the better part of the year.

His teeth chattered uncontrollably, and Gabriel just knew that his lips had turned blue. It had been drizzling constantly for the last quarter of an hour, and the rain had soaked him through.

Once he reached his destination, he stopped and wiped the water off his face with the back of his hand. At least, he had made it there.

Brushing unsteady fingers through the spikes of his hair, he looked up at the villas. No light showed in the windows.

He took shelter under the overhang of the cottage where he was supposed to sleep and lifted the bottle to his mouth, swallowing the potent liquid. The fire flickered in his stomach and spread everywhere in seconds.

He spent another hour there, relishing the fever that vodka built inside him. His mind meandered everywhere and nowhere. He lit a cigarette, and then another, until dizziness made him stop.

He studied the bottle through narrowed eyes and estimated that it still held a quarter more. He raised the bottle at his lips again, but nausea hit him hard, and he gagged.

"All right, all right," he muttered under his breath. "Tomorrow's another day. I'll finish it tomorrow."

It wasn't as if he had planned anything else to do the following day. When they got to the cabins, he had given each of his people papers outlining the plans for the following three days. They just snickered at him and balled the sheets, throwing them into the garbage.

Andy even made a show out of that, getting into Gabriel's face and challenging him to say something. Gabriel chose to keep his silence.

When he proposed to divide the team in two for a healthy game of volleyball in the afternoon, they had merely rolled their eyes and started filing out.

Their conversations revealed that they were going to look for a fast food shop or something. There was also a mention of a club for the evening. Of course, no one invited him to join them either.

Nonetheless, Gabriel had run out after them and shouted something about a hike up the mountain next day. He had also mentioned a competition and even advised them to go to bed early that evening. A few middle fingers had gone up in his face, and a couple of his people had even blessed him with a few choice words.

So there wouldn't be any hiking the following day. Nothing on his damn list would happen. He shrugged and resolved himself to go to bed, carrying his bottle with him.

Exhausted, Gabriel decided against climbing up the stairs to his bedroom and veered right toward the living room.

He imagined he could find the sofa without turning on the light. It was well after three a.m. anyway. He didn't want to drag his feet up the stairs and disturb anyone sleeping in the house, if someone was even there. They had probably gathered in the other villa just to get away from him.

He found the sofa after knocking into an armchair first and then into the corner of the coffee table. Sharp pain shot up his leg, and Gabriel drew air deeply into his lungs. He muttered, cursing his bad luck and his lack of attention.

His nostrils twitched at the acrid smell in the room, which turned his stomach upside down, and he clamped his teeth, wondering about the stench.

For a fleeting moment, he thought about finding the light switcher, but abandoned the idea. He knew that he would fall asleep instantly and forget about the smell, so he plopped onto the sofa, still holding the bottle close to his body.

He did fall asleep the moment his head touched the armrest and forgot about everything.

CHAPTER FIVE

Daylight filtered through the thin lacy curtains and tiptoed on Gabriel's eyelids, teasing him. The corners of his mouth twitched, and his eyelashes fluttered, but the man refused to wake up, even though wakefulness stirred at the edge of his mind. However, his colorful weird dreams receded and slid into nothingness, a pang of regret irritating the rational side of his brain.

His left arm curled over his eyes to hold off the light at bay. His bone-tired body begged for an hour more of unconscious bliss, but his deep breathing had already changed.

When Anna's ear-splitting screams rolled off the walls, Gabriel jumped out of bed, a groan off his lips. The vodka bottle, which was lying next to him over the slipcover, rolled down to the floor with a clatter.

"What the heck is going on? Why are you yelling like a lunatic?" Gabriel snapped at the young woman once he regained his feet under him.

He rubbed at the sand under his eyelids first and then massaged his aching temples for a couple of seconds. He soon realized that he needed more than that to overcome the din in the room, which tangled with the mother of all headaches pulsating behind his temples.

Annoyed, Gabriel ground his teeth and took a good look at Anna. The whiteness of her cheeks complemented the hue of the walls. Her eyes had widened, ready to jump out of their sockets, and the terror swimming in her pupils shook him.

"Stop with this infernal screeching and tell me what the problem is," he asked her in a harsh tone of voice, sure that she wouldn't shut up otherwise. Guilt for barking at an already distressed woman overwhelmed him.

Nevertheless, it worked. The young woman snapped her mouth shut and pointed a trembling finger toward the other side of the sofa. With dismay, Gabriel turned his eyes there. He expected to spy a mouse or a spider, and he felt like smacking one of the pillows over Anna's face.

Then, he paled instantly. He gagged and pressed the heel of his hand over his mouth, fervently wishing he wouldn't christen the living room. He didn't feel like cleaning afterward.

After a couple of seconds, the boiling in his belly subsided and became bearable. He lowered his hand from his mouth, regaining some of his usual cool.

The ice spreading in his body helped, even though it was getting in the way of his mind, and he could barely gather his thoughts.

Mia's battered face stared into his, the woman's mouth contorted in a cry. Her long fingers curled into the slipcover of the sofa. Her body bent over the armrest, her eyes turned to the door, and her long dark hair spilled on one side in a sea of soft waves. Gabriel had never touched her hair but still knew how it felt.

Gabriel's gaze roamed over the abused body, his mind turning around in a haze. However, his expression revealed nothing of what he was thinking or feeling.

He rubbed his stomach absently to calm it. Random thoughts popped into his head, and he didn't imagine they were worth the effort to hold on to them.

He mused if he was probably still sleeping or had been caught in a parallel universe. Murder was for books and had no part in his life.

Then, he shook his head at the slim body draped over the armrest. If he had fallen onto the couch the other way last night, he would have slept on top of the dead woman. The next thought told him that he was really screwed considering the circumstances.

Gabriel turned to Anna. She was weeping now, her head lowered in her hands and her shoulders shuddering. He closed his eyes for a second and shook his head again. Then, he said quietly, "Stop sniveling and go call the police now."

His calmness broke through the woman's terror. Anna wiped her clammy palms on her jeans and started to the kitchen where she had left her phone that morning. She hadn't made it to the door when Gabriel's words stopped her.

"No, that's not a good idea," he said, and the young woman turned around, surprise reflected in her eyes.

Gabriel might have behaved like a prick lately, but she had never taken him for a coward before. The man always faced up his responsibilities.

"I think I'd better not be left alone in here with the body but come with you," Gabriel continued in a matter-of-fact tone of voice.

He had noticed Anna's astonishment and had a good idea about what was going on in her mind. He reflected ruefully that it didn't matter. Mia alive would have meant some unpleasant moments and probably a fine sending off from the company.

That would have worked fine for him. He had already tiptoed around the idea of doing something else. On the other hand, Mia dead spelt big trouble, and probably a few years in the cage.

'*Who the heck would believe that I didn't kill her when I was found sleeping in the same room with her body? I wouldn't buy it myself.*'

"We should lock this door, as well," he said, pushing his fears aside and joining Anna at the door. "The police wouldn't like it if anyone messed around that... crime scene," he continued.

He led Anna toward the kitchen after turning the key in the lock and shoving it into his pants pocket.

He thought of going upstairs for a quick shower and a change of clothes, but nipped the idea in the bud. The police might have assumed that he had wanted to get rid of evidence. They were bound to think the worst of him anyway so he didn't need to give them more ammunition.

CHAPTER SIX

HIS HANDS DEEP IN HIS pockets, balancing on the balls of his feet, and filled with cautious and dread, Gabriel watched the proceedings from the threshold of the living room door. Several forensic techs crawled around, picking up one thing or another and bagging it.

The body had already been taken away to the morgue. The old coroner had exchanged a few quiet words with the person in charge and followed the corpse.

Gabriel hadn't thought that a lot could surprise him after that morning. Nonetheless, when his eyes fell on the person in charge, his brain shut down for a few seconds.

This one, an unexpectedly young woman, was moseying toward him right then, a little notebook secured in the curled fingers of her left hand, her step lazy and unhurried.

However, her determination came through the way she was pulling back her narrow shoulders, framed by a white shirt. That was what worried him. She looked willowy and delicate, but Gabriel doubted that he could find an indulgent bone in her body.

The woman meant business, he thought, and his mouth dried up. He rolled his tongue over his teeth and tasted tartness.

Dread had begun spreading inside his body ever since his gaze fell on Mia's battered body. Now it spiked up a notch.

He balled his hands into fists, satisfied that he had had the instinct to burrow them into his pockets. No one could witness his distress, and he was grateful for that.

The young woman, '*a chief inspector, imagine that,*' strode toward him, keeping her hazel eyes straight on his face. It unnerved him. He couldn't shake the feeling that the woman's gaze had already penetrated through his immobile features and uncovered most of his secrets.

Barely touching 5.2 feet, she walked like a straight arrow. Her thick dark hair plaited in a tight French braid reached the middle of her back. With her small, trim frame and her graceful gait, she was far from Gabriel's idea of a police inspector.

"Maybe we should find another room to talk," her voice smoothed over him, and Gabriel swallowed hard.

His amber eyes zeroed in on her mouth. Her lower full lip fascinated him, although he liked the other one as well.

"Sir?" she touched his arm when more than thirty seconds had passed, and he hadn't done anything else but stare at her.

The feel of her startled him, and his gaze shifted at her eyes, while embarrassment powdered his cheekbones pink. Gabriel searched frantically his mind for something to say and explain his behavior. He didn't want her to understand why he had spaced out, but he drew a blank. He gave up, and with a wide gesture, he showed her out of the room and into the hall.

"Let's go to the kitchen or onto the terrace, whatever you prefer," he invited her.

"Your friend is in the kitchen with Stefan," she informed him.

After a couple of seconds of puzzlement, he realized that she was talking about Anna who was just answering another inspector's questions.

"She's not my friend," he thought to mention. He didn't want to pile misunderstandings on top of his present problems.

When the woman arched her eyebrows, he understood that more explanations were in order.

"I'm her supervisor," he started to expound on his words, and one of those precisely defined eyebrows curved up. "We're here for team building exercises, and she's not the only one that's here with me," he added as he didn't want the inspector to nurture any wrong impressions.

"I see," she replied softly. "Where are the others then?" she asked him on their way to the terrace at the back of the villa.

"Probably in the other cottage," he shrugged her question as unimportant. *'How the hell should I know where they are? No one tells me anything around here,'* he reflected bitterly. 'But that's just fine. It doesn't matter,' he lied to himself, unwilling to dig deeper into his disappointment.

He shoved his hands in his pockets once more and clenched his fists. Right then, he didn't care even if his people had climbed the mountains at the back of the villas and hurled themselves over a ridge.

However, he couldn't stop wondering that no one had showed any curiosity as to what was going on in that cabin. Still baffled, he strode absently alongside the police inspector, his eyes on the highlands visible through the French doors leading out onto the terrace.

Once outside, they sat at the large lawn table surrounded by six chairs, Gabriel taking a seat across from the inspector. They looked one at the other for a few seconds, both trying to gauge the other one's thoughts.

Gabriel stretched his legs and took out a wrinkled pack of cigarettes from one of his roomy pockets and shook out a roll-up, satisfied that he had rolled enough cigs to last him for a few days. He wouldn't have had the patience to do it right then. Everything piled up on him, and he felt as if he had been teetering on the brink of an abyss.

The woman made note of the man's bloodshot eyes and the shadows under them. He didn't look like he had slept enough lately.

Then, she opened her notebook and braced her right hand on it, her long and elegant fingers playing with her pen.

"I didn't catch your name," she said, noting also the paleness of his skin and the deep lines around his mouth.

"You haven't asked," he replied smartly, and her eyes widened slightly at the cockiness in his voice.

The woman's lips twitched with repressed amusement, and she turned her head to the side, leaving the impression that she felt a sudden urge to admire the landscape.

Beyond the terrace, thick trees lined the pretense of a small flower garden, sparsely planted with a few petunias and pansies. No one had spared too much thought about it.

Farther away, the tree lines thickened up the hill, although not tidily, and spread up the mountain, to the calcareous rocks, which pierced the skyline.

"I'm asking now," her gaze returned to him once she was sure she wouldn't laugh.

"Gabriel Barna," he replied with a shrug.

"All right, Gabriel," she said, jotting his name down into her notebook.

"And yours?" Gabriel asked, admiring the tidy lines she scribbled on the paper.

"My what?" she looked up at him nonplussed.

"Your name, of course," he answered with a grin tucked at the corner of his mouth.

He knew what he was doing. He was merely courting more grief with his attitude, but that didn't mean that he could control his impulses.

She shook her head, not sure if his behavior should have offended or amused her.

"I told you my name when I came to the scene," she pointed out.

"I heard only that thing, Police Inspector or something," he explained, shaking his head. "It sounded so important that I forgot to pay attention to the name that followed after that."

"Oh, I see. It's Chief Inspector, and the name is Magda Luca," she replied. "You don't need to remember that Police Chief Inspector thing. Just Inspector will do," she offered.

"Magda's nice," Gabriel murmured softly, his eyes sweeping over the oval of her face, and then down over the white starched shirt, hiding the line of her small breasts.

"Might be, but it's not for you. I'm here on police business, not for a social visit," she pointed out, aiming a meaningful glance at him.

"Oh, yeah, indeed," Gabriel said with weary in his voice. His predicament had slipped his mind for a few minutes, and now the memory rushed back and slapped him at full impact.

"Now, could you tell me how you found the victim?" she asked him in a businesslike tone of voice, signaling that small talk had ended.

"Anna found her," he grumbled, a frown between his eyebrows. "I merely slept with her."

The words just slipped out of his mouth. When his mind processed what he had said, his eyes almost popped out of their sockets. He could have slapped himself over the head.

"Now... That's interesting, I'd say," the inspector murmured, targeting him with a razor-like gaze.

'*I just knew you'd think so,*' Gabriel grimaced with self-loathing.

"Maybe if you'd try to explain to me," Magda said, piercing him with a sharp gaze. "Do you mean that you used to sleep with the victim or what?"

"I have never slept with her," he replied. "At least not while she was alive," he thought to specify and clear any confusion.

"You'd be the first individual I've ever heard confessing that he slept with a dead woman," she said wryly, a stony expression on her face.

Suddenly, she didn't enjoy his cut and dry attitude anymore.

"If I remember correctly, and believe me, I do, there's an article in the criminal code that deals with that," she pointed out in a sharp tone of voice.

"Well, I didn't sleep with her that way. I just happened to fall asleep next to her," he clarified. "That doesn't fall anywhere under that criminal code article, I'm sure," he nodded wisely.

"How could someone just fall asleep next to a dead person?" she narrowed her eyes, a clear sign that she didn't believe his explanation.

"Someone could if that someone was drunk as a skunk," he shrugged.

Gabriel had decided to be open right from the beginning so he continued on the same line.

"I can't say that if I had known she was dead I'd have enjoyed having such an experience. Anyway, I just didn't know that the body was there."

He shook his head with dismay, cursing his stupid big mouth, which used to run away, instead of staying in sync with his mind. He wanted to be truthful, but that didn't mean to be an idiot, though.

Irritated, he tapped his cigarette in the ashtray on the table, although he had hardly managed to draw two smokes out of it. It had just burnt by itself.

"Luckily, if I can use the term," he grimaced, "I wasn't aware that I fell asleep next to a dead woman. When I found out, the fact already belonged in the past," he opened his arms widely.

However, he knew that he would never be able to forget about that. He still shuddered when he recalled Mia's abused body on the sofa.

Magda stared at the man before her eyes and analyzed him carefully. Then she nodded and scribbled a few notes in her notebook.

"Now I understand why there's blood on your jeans," she pointed her forefinger toward the cuff of his pants.

Gabriel lowered his gaze and lifted his feet to have a look for himself. When his eyes found the spots of blood, he swore viciously and began to rub his stomach absently with a gesture that had already become habit for him.

He hadn't noticed the blood before. Now that he knew of its presence, the nausea hit him once more. He swallowed hard a couple of times to keep it at bay and shut his eyes tight, avoiding to look up at Magda until he had regained his cool back.

"I understand you were drunk when you came in last night," Magda said, folding her hands on her notebook. "Still, could you estimate when you got to the living room?"

Gabriel leaned back in his chair and made a few hasty calculations in his head. Then, his mouth sketched a pitiful grin, and he shook his head.

"I'm afraid I can't," he replied. "Probably somewhere after midnight, I think. Long after midnight," he corrected his statement and patiently waited for the next question.

He was aware that he couldn't talk his way out of that mire if she wasn't the type of inspector who wanted to make sure that she got the right man for the crime.

Her steady searching gaze troubled him. This woman seemed capable to see inside him, and he didn't feel comfortable with that. A shiver ran along his back, and his eyes turned to the peaks in the distance.

"Fair enough, I'd say," she murmured.

She watched the play of expressions on the man's face with concealed amusement, imagining that he would have liked to appear mysterious and unreadable. He was playing it cool, but he couldn't hide his fear and shock. She found him interesting enough to dig more.

"I'd like you to explain to me how you all got here and why," she invited him with a wide wave of her hand.

"By train," he replied without turning to her.

"Being flippant doesn't help," Magda returned in a soft, warning voice, feeling that she could get more out of him with softness. However, she reserved the right of tearing into him if it became necessary.

"I'm not flippant," he said, snapping to attention. "We came by train, indeed."

"You know very well that's not what I asked," she tossed back, trying for patience, even though her back was up now.

"If you say so," Gabriel murmured and shifted his position in the chair.

The inspector's eyebrows arched, and her reproachful glaze scorched him. Gabriel shoved his hands into his pockets again and tried for an indifferent look.

"All right, I'll tell you. My manager decided on this trip. Something along the lines of a team building, you know. We've built the team, indeed," he observed, his voice filled with harsh irony.

"What do you mean?" Magda leaned forward, bracing her forearms on the table and watching him attentively.

"We lost one member of the team yesterday or early this morning, didn't we?" he shrugged. "Not that it was much of a team to begin with," he muttered under his beard.

"Meaning?" she asked, proving to him that her ears worked just fine.

"Meaning that the team is in shambles," he replied in a harsh tone of voice. "I've lost any authority and respect I held before, you know," he shrugged again, and this time his face did become unreadable.

"You lost them during this trip?" she inquired, watching him from under her lashes.

"Nah, long before the trip," he admitted, shaking his head with a pang of guilt. "The trip was just the final straw," he said, shifting his eyes toward the forest.

He breathed in deeply, to calm the anxiety humming in his body. A light breeze sang through the leaves of the trees, and beams of light glittered here and there, soothing his eyes.

"I see... Would you care to explain why?" Magda asked, busying her eyes with dissecting him.

He took a few moments to think about that and to find an excuse or another. After a couple of minutes, he gave up and decided to go with the truth.

"Poor management, I'd say," he shrugged the question away. "More specifically, my poor management... Poor choices... The usual, you know," he admitted, turning his gaze back to her and looking straight into her eyes.

"What about the woman dead in the living room?" the inspector asked, leaning back in her lawn chair and tilting her head to the side in order to judge the witness's behavior better.

"Mia Lazar," he specified. "That's her name, but I suppose you already know that. She persuaded me to bring her to the department from another project."

He shifted his gaze back to the forest, knowing that his eyes would change with the following words. He didn't want Magda to see that.

"And then?" Magda inquired quietly.

"Then she convinced the other team leader to move her to my team," he shrugged, looking straight into the policewoman's eyes now. He didn't even blink.

"Why?" the next question came.

For a few seconds, Gabriel just looked at the woman sitting across from him. Then, an ugly smile lit his face, giving her a jolt.

"Probably because she had never intended to go out with me," he said boldly, taking his hands out of his pockets and crossing his arms over his chest. "She just strung me along, you know."

"Now, that's interesting, I'd say," Magda murmured, her eyes narrowing and assessing him with more care.

She tried hard not to whistle. Here, she had one of the primary reasons that led men to kill women. It was just text book homicide. She could have just tied the case with a bow and be done with it. However, she had some difficulty in seeing Gabriel in the role of a killer, but she had uncovered stranger things before.

"So there's some history between the two of you," she drew the conclusion just to see what his answer would be.

"If you choose to look at things like that, then yes, there's some history," Gabriel shrugged.

He fidgeted in his chair, uneasy under her wary gaze, and then he crossed his ankles and lit another cigarette, slightly amused to notice that his hands seemed steady enough.

"And how would you look at them?" Magda tilted her head, watching him inquiringly.

"Something on the lines '*Let's catch a sucker*,'" he shrugged, but couldn't quite meet her eyes.

Admitting the truth embarrassed him. He hadn't discussed that part with anyone until that moment.

"And here I'd have thought that I was smarter than that," he shook his head with scorn.

"Would you care to elaborate?" she arched her eyebrows, waiting for him to look at her so that she could read him better.

"Not much to say," he shook his head. "But I suppose I have to," he shifted his eyes toward her, a bashful grin in the corner of his mouth.

"Pretty much, yes, you do," she nodded, and he grimaced.

She needed to fight back a smile. He looked like a rebellious teenager, in spite of his age. The light in his amber eyes glimmered with resistance.

"Then I'll tell you," he turned toward her completely now, determined to clear the air.

He fussed a bit, looking for a more comfortable position, and then started to talk.

"I met her at work. She used to work in a different department, you know, but we bumped into each other in the smoking area several times," he said.

He breathed deeply and then drew a long smoke from his cigarette. His eyes wandered toward the trees, but then returned to her.

"Anyway, we chatted for a few days... Actually, I should say that she chatted me up for a few days," he scowled, and the wrinkle between his eyebrows deepened more.

"I see," Magda murmured, and her hazel eyes turned richer. "You mean that she played her role well and turned your head."

"See, you've caught onto that sooner than I did," he bit out with bitterness.

Then he chuckled, grasping the irony of the situation. He shook his head with self-contempt, and his lips became a thin line.

"So, in a nutshell, she chatted you up," Magda summed the situation.

Gabriel nodded, searching her eyes to guess what she was thinking.

"You wouldn't have been the first or the last to go through something like that, would you?" her eyes sparkled.

"It wasn't as simple as that," he defended himself, his fingers drumming onto the top of the lawn table.

"What complicated matters?" Magda arched her brows.

"She convinced me to help her move into my department," he confessed.

"So office romance is acceptable in your company?" the inspector inquired, her tone of voice betraying her disbelief.

"There aren't clear rules, you know," Gabriel waved widely. "There are a lot of gray areas. Of course, it is expected not to… romance, let's say, someone in your own team if you're the one in charge," he explained with a shrug.

"Then how come she… flirted with you in order to persuade you to bring her into your department? That doesn't really make sense, does it now?" Magda stared at him, her eyes two narrow slits.

"The plan wasn't to bring her in my team. There are two teams in the department. She was supposed to go to the other team, so we could have a hot steamy affair," Gabriel replied with derision in his voice.

"So what happened then?" Magda asked, caught in the story by now.

"I brought her in. I don't know what she did or what she said, but the other team leader dumped her in my team," he explained, waving his hands widely. "Of course, that was what Mia had planned from the beginning, you know," he said and exhaustion crept in his voice.

Magda leaned back in her chair, tapping her pen onto her notebook. Gabriel seemed lost in thought, so she took her time to really look at him.

The man looked pretty wasted, even though he had caught a few hours of sleep. The shadows and planes of his face set out the molten amber of his eyes, and the cynical lines around his mouth could make a woman feel on the edge.

"A few weeks ago, I found out that she actually had a boyfriend. She'd been in that relationship for the latter part of the year, to be precise," he started talking again and turned to her. "It started long before she corralled me."

The grin had disappeared, and the hard set of his lips left no doubt of how deeply he felt about what had happened.

Magda didn't know if serious feelings had been involved, or only his pride had been bruised, but it seemed that he had several motives to pay Mia back.

"I see," Magda murmured her eyes always on the man's face. "You realize that you've just told me that you had plenty reasons to wish her dead."

"I know, but I doubt that you wouldn't uncover everything by yourself. So there's no point in keeping secrets, is there?" he scowled at her.

Magda's lips twitched with unconcealed humor, drawing Gabriel's eyes. He didn't bother to hide his fascination with her little bow mouth, perfectly framed in a face sculptured with delicacy and flair.

All features went along with each other, and he couldn't isolate the slightest flaw. Gabriel couldn't remember to have ever seen such an exquisite specimen of womanhood.

She left the impression of being delicate and graceful, but that didn't dupe him. He could spy strength and stubbornness beneath all that cool beauty.

"Right, there's no point in keeping secrets," Magda agreed with him.

He perceived the amusement in her voice but decided not to react. He didn't have the right to complain. Anybody would laugh their ass off when faced with an idiot of such a magnitude.

"So what happened afterward?" Magda asked, crossing her legs, and playing with the pen in her hand.

"She got into the department. As I said, within just two days, she made the other team leader to move her into my team. She knew I couldn't pursue an affair with her if she was my subordinate," he recited in a toneless voice and shrugged.

"So, was that all?" Magda arched one eyebrow, stopping her playing with the pen.

Gabriel gazed at her, sarcasm flickering in his pupils. He shook his head, and took a moment to think.

He knew that what he was going to say would hammer the last nail to his coffin. However, keeping it secret would make everything look even worse.

"Of course not," his tongue snaked out to wet his dry lips. "Once she got into my team, she started doing whatever she wanted. One thing was clear. She didn't feel like working at all."

"What did you do?" Magda inquired, stilling her fingers when they started drumming the pen onto the top of the lawn table.

"Called a meeting to explain what she was supposed to do..." he shrugged.

Magda realized that shrugging seemed ingrained to his personality.

"How did that go? The meeting, I mean."

"Just swell," he laughed with derision. "She told me to back off, or she would complain that I sexually harassed her."

"That's... an interesting reaction," Magda managed to say.

"Yeah, that's what I thought as well," Gabriel replied with sarcasm.

"So what did you do?" Magda wanted to know.

"Nothing," he confessed. "I just backed off."

"For how long?" the inspector asked, feeling that the man she had before her eyes wouldn't have been able to hold back for long.

"Not long, just a few months. Nevertheless, that was enough to break the team," he admitted, his eyes on the skyline.

"So what did you do after those few months?" she asked again.

"I did what I had to do," he muttered, shifting his gaze toward the forest again.

He rubbed his temples for a couple of seconds, and then looked back at Magda.

"You'll find out soon enough so I'd better tell you," he said quietly but didn't continue. He merely gazed at her, shoving his hands into his pockets once more.

"Tell me what?" she asked, gazing at him intently. She could feel he was tense and anxious.

He shrugged, looked for the right words and drew a blank, so he blurted out the truth.

"She did file a complaint for sexual harassment against me. Next Monday, I am supposed to appear before a commission because of that," he explained in a monotone tone of voice.

"Another reason for you to kill her," she noted thoughtfully, tapping the pen over her lips.

He chuckled bitterly. "Yes, you could say that," he acknowledged the truth, taking his hands out of his pockets and opening his arms. "You're probably satisfied. You've nailed the case faster than you'd have thought," he remarked coldly.

"Not particularly," she shook her head, studying him. "There's still some research to do," she pointed out.

Gabriel merely shrugged. Either he didn't have any interest in her words, or he didn't believe her.

"Would you give us the clothes you're having on you right now?" the woman asked, tilting her head to the side to better study him. "And I mean everything you're wearing."

"Yeah, you can have everything you want," he said.

A slightly amused light flickered in his eyes while considering her.

"Should I take everything off right now?" he asked, his voice daring her.

"No, thank you, I'll pass on the thrill," she replied dryly. "I will send Stefan with you upstairs. You'll peel the clothes off you, and he'll bag them."

"Too bad," Gabriel shook his head. "I liked my idea better. At least I'd have gotten something out of it," he winked, even though it was obvious that his mind wasn't quite into that.

"I'm sure you would," Magda nodded with empathy. "But I'm not here to make things thrilling for you, you know."

"Hadn't imagined you were," he replied, his features hardened now. "Any more questions?" he asked her, his head held high and a dangerous light in his eyes.

Magda pressed her lips, thinking of a scorching reply. Annoyance shone in her eyes, and her right foot tapped the tiles of the terrace, betraying her upset. She had just opened the mouth to scold him when Anna strode onto the terrace.

"I'm sorry to disturb," she smiled weakly at both of them. Her features were tense, and she was rubbing her hands together, full of anxiety.

"What now?" Gabriel asked, a bit of frost in his voice.

He didn't feel too charitable toward anyone right then. His very freedom hung in the balance, and he didn't have a clue what to do in order to protect it.

"No one knows where Alex is. Victor, Dan and George said that they haven't seen him since yesterday afternoon. The others are all on the veranda in front of the villa," she pointed her chin toward the inside of the house.

Gabriel just stared at Anna nonplussed. Magda turned to him and assessed his facial expressions with interest. Annoyance and impatience warred with disbelief both in his eyes and the line of his lips.

"Are you sure he didn't hook up with someone?" he asked after a few moments of tense silence.

Anna had already started fidgeting, uncomfortable under his stare.

Gabriel didn't know what to believe, but he didn't think anyone should worry about Alex. He was known as a ladies' man, and would always pick up girls faster than anybody else he knew. That was why Gabriel inclined to believe that the guy was holed up somewhere with a woman.

However, Anna shook her head to contradict him, even if she seemed reluctant to do it.

"I don't think so. He was upset with you and didn't feel like spending time with us. After he drank two beers, he said he'd come back here. None of us has seen him ever since," she said.

"Have you checked all the rooms in the other villa?" Gabriel inquired, and Anna nodded at once. "What about the rooms in this one?" he asked again.

"We haven't checked here yet," she admitted. "We thought to ask you first. Maybe you've seen him somewhere, and we were just fussing. Since you haven't, I think we should start checking the rooms upstairs," she replied. "He isn't down here," she pointed out. "He'd have come out by now."

"That's true," Gabriel concurred with her. "Let's see if he's upstairs then," he started toward the door.

"All right, then," Magda said from behind him. "I will be waiting here and have a few words with Stefan."

Gabriel had already reached the stairs with huge steps. He didn't turn but just waved his hand to show that he had heard her. He continued climbing up to the first floor, Anna in his wake.

Once he reached the landing, he took the corridor to the right and went directly to the room Alex should have shared with Andy.

The latter had chosen that bedroom because of its position. It was the room farthest from Gabriel's, which lay at the other end of the passageway. It occupied a secluded recess and didn't share the bathroom with another room, although it didn't have a bathtub. A shower stand worked just fine for Andy.

Gabriel knocked on the door and waited for an answer. After a couple of seconds, he pushed the door open and surveyed the room. Bags had been scattered around, and clothes had spilled out of them and spread over the floor and chairs. Nevertheless, it was obvious that no one had slept in either of the beds.

Gabriel strode inside the room and went to the bathroom, whose door had been left wide open. His eyes swept over the dry sink and undisturbed towels. There wasn't any sign that anyone had visited that room for several hours.

"He's not here," Gabriel returned to the door where Anna was waiting for him. "We'll check all the rooms," he decided, although the thought that shouting Alex's name might put a faster end to the search floated in his mind.

Followed by Anna, Gabriel started throwing doors open and searching every room on the landing, as well as the adjacent bathrooms. His patience was wearing thin, and he promised himself to tear into Alex for making him behave like an idiot.

"He's not in the house," Anna's anxious voice penetrated Gabriel's thought. "There's only your room left," she said, and Gabriel's sharp gaze turned to her.

He didn't think that she had noticed which one was his room. He remembered what Adam had said, and the man's words started making sense, making him ill in the process.

"We'll check my room, too," Gabriel replied curtly. "I don't see Alex finding refuge in my room, but we'd better be thorough," he explained, his huge steps eating the length of the hall.

He opened the door to his room and stepped inside. The open door of the bathroom offered a clear line of sight inside that room, and Gabriel understood that no one was there.

He took a step inside the room. The door had hidden the bed under the window from sight, but now that his eyes fell on it, he drew a sharp breath into his lungs.

He swallowed hard, and his insides quivered. His chin fell to his chest while he acknowledged that he had run out of chances and would certainly see the inside of a prison. He would have years to become acquainted with that life.

"I'll come out and lock this door now, Anna," he said in an eerie, calm tone of voice. "I will wait here on the landing. You go and bring the police upstairs."

Anna's hand flew at her throat, and she asked in a small voice, "Is Alex in there, Gabriel?"

"Yes, he is," Gabriel replied, in the same remote and strange voice. "Look, listen, Anna," he came out of the room, closing the door behind him so that the young woman didn't see what lay on the bed.

He didn't think that he could have kept his cool if she had started screaming like earlier in the day.

"Look, Anna, I'm locking the door," he turned the key into the lock with a wide and theatrical gesture.

"You take the key," he handed her the key swiftly, so that he wouldn't change his mind.

It was too tempting, his survival instincts pulling at him and trying to make him do something stupid.

"Now I'll be leaning here on the banister. You go and bring that police woman upstairs," he asked her in a soft tone of voice, a forced grin hovering at the corner of his mouth.

Then, burrowing his hands into his pockets, he leaned on the railing, crossing his ankles.

Anna looked at him with sad, puppy eyes. After a couple of seconds, she nodded with some uncertainty and started descending the stairs.

She kept turning around and looking at him. Tears welled in her eyes, and Gabriel knew that she understood that he didn't have a prayer to get out of that jam.

CHAPTER SEVEN

The morgue techs took the bagged body out of the room, and Magda followed them with the coroner. Her head tilted to the old man with interest.

They seemed to be discussing something intently. However, they kept their voices so low that Gabriel couldn't catch a word.

Once the coroner took the stairs down, Magda turned to Gabriel.

"We need to talk some more," she said, and Gabriel nodded. "First, you should borrow some clothes from one of your guys," she waved toward the cluster of people at the foot of the stairs.

Gabriel followed her gestures and noticed Andy, moving to and fro, his fists clenching and unclenching. Gabriel wouldn't have been surprised to see tears in the big guy's eyes.

Alex had been Andy's best friend and the man who had brought him into the team. Gabriel remembered that Andy and Alex had known each other for over ten years. In spite of the difference in age, the two of them had run in the same circle, and their connection had been strengthened with the passing of time.

"I doubt anyone would give me anything," Gabriel muttered, turning back to Magda. "I suppose you could choose some pants and a tee from my bag. I'll go commando so I don't have to trouble you with choosing underwear," he grinned mischievously.

Although she had met him only that morning, Magda already knew that he chose to show that callous mask whenever he felt threatened. She shook her head and returned into his bedroom.

"Adrian, could you find a pair of jeans or something and a tee in that bag? Something the owner could wear without obstructing the investigation," her musical voice filled the hall.

"I suppose so," a man replied. "It doesn't look like he unzipped this bag at all any time before the murder or after," he remarked. "See the splatters here. There's nothing inside, just a drop that licked through the links of the zipper."

After a couple of minutes, Magda returned with some slacks and a t-shirt. She handed them to Gabriel and called for Stefan, advising him to bring a bag for evidence. When Stefan came out of Gabriel's bedroom, she showed them to another room.

"Let him change his clothes and take into evidence everything he's wearing," she said, and Stefan nodded.

He waved his hand to show Gabriel to go inside the room before him, and then he followed.

"I'll be downstairs on the terrace," Magda shouted after them.

Stefan waved his hand to show that he understood, and Gabriel just muttered something unintelligible under his breath.

Gabriel stripped down in front of the policeman and stretched his hand to take the slacks and pull them up. He fastened his pants, and then pulled his t-shirt, his eyes following Stefan's movements.

The policeman packed everything with precise and measured gestures, jamming the clothes into the evidence bag. Then, he zipped it, the sound grating on Gabriel's nerves and bloating his fear.

He didn't know if anything on his clothes could point the finger to him as the criminal, and he hated his impotence. He couldn't do a damn thing to clear his name.

"Let's go downstairs," the policeman said, his green eyes piercing Gabriel's. "Magda is not very patient on her good days, and you wouldn't like to get on her bad side," he advised, without a trace of smile.

A few years older and a head taller than Gabriel, the man exuded brute force and inflexibility. His immobile features and broken nose advertised his ruggedness.

Still, Gabriel preferred his steely look to Magda's softness. He had stopped trusting his first impressions when it came to women, and he refused to be made a fool once more.

"Should I lead the way?" Gabriel asked in a mocking tone of voice, and Stefan arched an eyebrow.

The man didn't seem to appreciate Gabriel's levity but didn't bother to answer. He merely continued to pin the younger man with his penetrating stare, making him squirm.

"All right, I see that's what you'd prefer," Gabriel shrugged as if the policeman's attitude hadn't had the power to touch him, and his upper lip curled.

He despised himself. His spine had turned into jelly since that morning. Nevertheless, the policeman's attitude didn't leave room to interpretations. If he had been in charge, Gabriel would have already been arrested and behind bars.

Shuddering inwardly with dread, Gabriel left the room and climbed down the stairs, Stefan's steps crowding him with their staccato on the wooden steps. Gabriel ground his teeth and pursed his lips with determination. He had already been scared to the marrow so he refused to give in another inch.

He stepped onto the terrace with a brisk stride and stopped in his tracks abruptly when he spotted Magda questioning Anna. The latter was crying in earnest, and the scene set Gabriel's teeth on edge. He could only imagine what stories Anna was telling the inspector.

For a second, hatred filled his chest and eyes, and Magda, who had just looked up at him, almost jumped out of her skin. There was an entire fountain of negative feelings in Gabriel's eyes.

That kind of hatred would have made his fingers curl around Anna's neck and throttle her. Still, the man quenched that loathing almost instantly, and the amber of his eyes turned remote and disinterested.

"Should I come back later?" he asked, although he felt Stefan at his back, ready to push him forward if he did well on his words.

"No, it's not necessary," Magda's reply came in a cool tone of voice. She stood up with a slow movement, her fingers turning a page in her notebook absently.

Gabriel's upper lip curled, while his eyes glinted under the tawny eyelashes that snapped together. He had read her gesture correctly. The inspector didn't want him to have a look at her notes.

"Anna and I have just finished talking," Magda stroked her fingers gently over the distressed young woman's shoulder.

Anna jumped out of her chair, understanding that she was expected to leave. She brushed her tears away with the tips of her fingers, and rushed by Gabriel, her head down, swallowing guiltily.

For an instant, the man's eyes rested on the top of her head, and then swept over the hands she was clenching around her midriff. He shook his head with sadness. He had never looked at Anna with the eyes of a man. However, he cared for her in his way and didn't like to see her so distraught.

A fleeting smile appeared on Magda's lips, and one of her eyebrows arched. The man was full of contradiction, an interesting conundrum in himself.

Her instincts pointed into a different direction than Gabriel's for the killer, but she still needed to do her job. She couldn't solve a murder with instincts. She needed proof and explanations that stood up in a court of law.

Magda looked beyond Gabriel toward Stefan and noticed that his brows knitted. The man had already drawn his own conclusions, and they were on a collision course with hers.

"Stefan, there are a few people gathered in the kitchen and outside the cottage. Could you start the interviews with them, please?"

The policeman nodded. However, his eyes showed his dissatisfaction with the way she understood to conduct that investigation. Magda grinned at him unconcerned.

It wasn't the first time that they had been on different wavelengths. She imagined that was the reason they had been paired up from the beginning. Being so dissimilar, nothing could get past them. One of them was bound to see something if the other overlooked it.

Once Stefan left the terrace, Magda invited Gabriel to sit down and answer her questions. Noticing that he was rubbing his stomach unconsciously, she asked, "Are you hungry? I suppose you haven't had breakfast today, and it's already well over noon."

He waved her assumption away. "No worries. I'll probably grab something to eat after you finish your interrogation. I'll go out into town for an hour or so, if you don't arrest me. If you do, then I suppose that I'm out of luck. I believe that lunch hour has already come and gone in jail," he attempted to joke, but his voice sounded flat.

"I think we can skip taking you into custody for the moment," the reply came. "I don't prance around arresting people without definite evidence in hand," Magda said in a deadpan voice.

"Lucky me," Gabriel murmured and stretched his legs in front of him, bracing his elbows on the table. "So ask," he flipped his fingers.

"There's no question that you knew the second victim as well," she noted.

"No, there's not. Alex started working in my team about two years ago... And he was good, damn good, if you need to know," he replied, sadness creeping in his voice.

"You were friends," the inspector concluded, watching the unshed tears gathered in his eyes.

"Not lately," he shook his head with regret. "But we were before everything started going downhill."

"I hear that you had a row two days ago," Magda probed, tilting her head.

"I see that Anna has been busy telling stories," he mused, and a line appeared between his brows. "Yes, we had a row two days ago. We've had several rows lately. What's the point of rehashing all that? I've already told you about my team," he glowered. "I didn't kill Alex, and I didn't kill Mia," he slammed his fist on the table, sick of having to tiptoe around that matter.

"I don't know that yet," Magda replied unconcerned with his temper. "You'll have to help me get there," she pointed out, looking straight into his troubled eyes.

'Look here," he started in force and then closed his eyes for a couple of seconds. He pursed his lips, and then, with determination, continued, "I had problems with everyone on the team. I know that Mia made a complaint to HR. I've already told you that."

Magda nodded to show her assent, but didn't reply. She was too busy assessing the man's inner turmoil.

"You've probably already found out that Alex made a complaint as well... For lack of fairness or something like that, I think. That should have been discussed next week as well. But let's be honest here…" he opened his arms, leaning back in his chair. "How many people start killing their colleagues because of a complaint to HR?"

"Well, it depends on the complaint," Magda shrugged. "I'd say that a complaint for sexual harassment might lead to a crime, considering your history with Mia," she tapped her pen on the top of her notebook.

"All right, let's say that. However, Alex's complaint shouldn't have led to crime. Come on, it's a petty reason, and I am not so stupid," he argued his opinion, and his forehead furrowed.

"I don't know you. I don't know what makes you tick," Magda countered. "I can go with only what I can see," she lifted one shoulder, licking her lower lip.

Gabriel followed the tip of her tongue wetting the lush surface of her lip, and he stuck his upper lip between his teeth. Then, he shook his head to clear it. He had more serious things to consider than how luscious her mouth looked.

"All right, you don't know, and you have to go with what you see. I wonder how you don't see that you could look at this entire story from a different angle," he said in a querulous tone of voice.

"Enlighten me," she replied matter-of-factly.

"Two people I had beef with have just died. Someone murdered them, and in quite an ugly manner. Shouldn't that show that someone has something against me and wants me to pay for that?"

"That thought crossed my mind," she replied mildly. "Still, that doesn't mean that you are off the hook. With how many other people in these two cottages did you have a quarrel with?"

He laughed mirthlessly, and shook his head. He looked over her head toward the horizon, and after a few more seconds, his eyes returned to her.

"All of them?" he said in a slightly interrogative tone of voice.

"So, if your theory is correct, any one of them could be the next victim, and at the same time, any one of them could be our killer," her eyes bored into him.

Gabriel took a moment to think and then nodded.

"Yeah, I think you nailed it. How do we make sure that no one else dies?" he asked, and the underlying toughness in his voice surprised Magda.

She scrutinized him for so long that it seemed like ages. He fought the urge to fidget under her gaze, and kept his eyes on her.

"You could move out from here," she said after a while. "Of course, you can't go back home. You have to stay here for the moment, at least another day or two," she pointed out.

"All right, I'll check in somewhere. I saw several bed and breakfasts around. What about my team? Shouldn't they go back home?" he inquired.

She shook her head at once. "Not right now. If you're telling the truth, and you're not the killer, one of them is. I can't let them go just now."

"Fair enough," he grumbled. "I suppose I can't take my things," he said. "However, I will need my documents and money to go somewhere else," he explained.

"Yes, you will. I will have Stefan bring them to you.

Gabriel strode to the French doors but turned back to Magda after a few steps. He noticed the interrogation in her eyes and shook his head.

"I just wanted to say," he started and then licked his lips.

He looked over her head for a few seconds, clenching his right fist, and then continued, "Well, you can take Andy out of the equation."

Magda raised her brows and looked at him inquiringly.

Gabriel breathed deeply and said, "Andy's bond with Alex was very strong. You could say that it was unbreakable. He couldn't have killed Alex," he shook his head. "And Anna... I doubt she has it in her... Killing, I mean."

Magda pursed her lips and watched him pensively. Then, she nodded, "I will think on that. But you don't know how many people kill someone they love, and how many people who wouldn't kill a fly would murder someone just for the heck of it," she offered him as a parting shot.

CHAPTER EIGHT

Gabriel lounged in a lawn chair on the quaint terrace of the bed and breakfast where he had taken up quarters the day before after leaving the villas and his team in the hands of the police. Well, he hadn't had a choice there, he shrugged.

He nursed a coffee so stiff that the hair at the back of his neck bristled. A permanent glower pulled the corners of his mouth down, and his brows knitted.

The deep shadows under his eyes proved that he hadn't enjoyed too much sleep the previous night either, so he had covered them with his dark sunglasses.

He scowled at the thought of having slept about four hours a night lately and wondered how long he could go on that way. Well, not very long, for sure. Exhaustion had already caught up with him.

His mood as black as the coffee in his mug, Gabriel tried to make sense of what had happened to Mia and Alex, drumming his fingers on the square table covered with a red and yellow tablecloth.

He shouldn't have cared about Mia, but he did. Despite her less than shining personality, she had been a human being, and a young one at that. Life should have stretched before her, no matter how she chose to live it.

Mia's death made him sad. Alex's ripped his heart out. The man had been one of the few through-and-through decent people in the world. His big heart hadn't allowed pettiness and hadn't known the meaning of hatred.

Gabriel had always made a point of not letting his tears fall, no matter of what life thought of throwing at him. Still, during the previous night, he had mourned the man who deserved so much and got so little out of his brief existence.

Crying hadn't felt demeaning or prissy in the solitude of his room. It had cleared some of Gabriel's thoughts and helped with some decisions he wouldn't have made otherwise.

Grieving deeply, on top of everything else, Gabriel would have preferred to bury his head somewhere in the sand and forget about everything. Even so, he had tried to reach Adam several times the previous afternoon and inform him about what had happened to the team.

He couldn't go around that. He hadn't probably been much of a team leader lately, and he would be the first to admit it. However, it didn't sit well with him to let Adam hear the news from someone else.

Yet, Adam had never returned any of his calls. Probably, he had been caught in meetings all day long and hadn't finished work until very late in the night. The man had very strange notions about what weekend meant.

In the end, annoyed that his calls kept going unanswered, Gabriel had left a cryptic message in Adam's voicemail and now waited for his call back. As a rule, Adam never set work aside, even on a Sunday, so Gabriel didn't think that he had to wait for a long time.

Still turning everything in his mind and analyzing every aspect of the situation, Gabriel's gaze fell on a young stout woman who strode out onto the terrace. She carried a tray piled up with his choices for breakfast. He had been so peculiar with his order that the waitress barely managed to write it down, while staring at him dumbfounded.

Apparently, people didn't have such an appetite first thing in the morning. Gabriel had had enough time to work one up.

The man sat up in his chair, his mood suddenly improved, and a smile widened on his face when the smell of fried bacon tickled his nostrils. He was famished as he had eaten close to nothing the day before.

His stomach had revolted at the smell of food, so he hadn't dared to swallow more than a few bites during his late lunch. Even so, he had lost most of that getting sick in his bathroom afterward, and he had been happy that he made it in there.

Later, concerned that he couldn't keep anything down, as he had surprisingly found out after his lunch, Gabriel had skipped dinner altogether. Instead, he had wandered for hours, hoping that he would forget for a while about the bleakest day of his life. Yet, that hadn't worked well either. Some images were burnt on his retina.

Gabriel expressed his gratitude for the waitress's effort with a boyish smile, which didn't really reach his eyes. However, what she didn't see couldn't hurt her.

He complimented the woman so profusely that she blushed violently. His words flattered and intimidated her to the point that she practically overturned the serving dish crowded with bacon, eggs and pieces of sausages.

Gabriel's eyes darkened beneath the concealing lenses, and the man shut up. He regretted his effusion and feared that he would miss the chance to dig his teeth into the succulent meat, still sizzling on the platter.

After busying herself with arranging the various dishes on the table before him, the woman left him alone with his breakfast and returned back to the kitchen. Even so, she kept turning her eyes back, gaping at him and shaking her head.

Gabriel didn't spare a gaze for her. He merely attacked his eggs and bacon, pushing his already cold coffee aside with a hurried gesture, while his stomach wept with joy at the sight of the plentiful meal.

When the woman returned and offered a refill for his coffee mug, he nodded eagerly, but then, he was already halfway through his breakfast. The smell of freshly brewed coffee made his nose twitch, and he inhaled it greedily.

A pleased smile on her lips, the waitress filled his cup to the rim, and with a brief baffled headshake, she left once more, certain that she had never seen someone so ravenous as their new customer.

Though delighted with the fresh refill, Gabriel didn't stop chewing. He continued shoveling food into his mouth as if he hadn't eaten for days. His taste buds stirred, and the juicy meat wetted the inside of his cheeks.

Gabriel enjoyed the tastes and textures, but he also knew that he needed all his neurons fired up in order to find a solution and get out of that gloomy situation. Food would help with that as well as coffee.

He had always had to do everything by himself whenever he needed something, so he wouldn't count on anyone to support him. Rules were rules, and he'd better stick to them.

Putting his fate in someone else's hands, even though the policewoman seemed fair enough, went against all his principles. Besides, it wasn't a piece of cake having a murder attached to his name. However, two crimes flirted with disaster and ridicule at the same time.

Gabriel had barely finished his breakfast and lit a roll-up to enjoy his fresh coffee when his mobile phone rang. A brief gaze at the screen told him that Adam had finally decided to check his messages.

"Hi there, Adam," Gabriel greeted his boss in a serious tone of voice.

"You don't sound like a man enjoying a few days in the mountains, everything paid for by the company, by the way," Adam retorted. "What's wrong?"

Gabriel chuckled warily, and drew another smoke of his cig. He then pushed the smoke out of his strained lungs and said, "Maybe it would be easier to tell you what's not wrong."

"Man, I didn't think you had it in you to botch a team building action," Adam replied in his hard voice, and Gabriel could very nearly see the glint in those hard eyes and the man's headshake of disappointment.

"It's way beyond botching right now," Gabriel admitted ruefully.

"How come? What do you mean?" Adam's firm voice inquired, and a sense of dread overwhelmed Gabriel.

"Well, if I were to tell you that I've already lost two of the team..."

"Where did you lose them?" Adam interrupted him with impatience, and Gabriel started counting to keep his cool. "Have you lost them on the mountain? How the heck could you have done that?" the man shouted.

Gabriel winced, fearing that his hearing wouldn't ever be the same. Adam had two perfectly functioning lungs, and he wasn't afraid to use them.

"It was your duty to make sure everyone came back in one piece," Adam pointed out, really pissed off with Gabriel now. "Have you called the mountain rescue services? Or probably you are waiting for me to do it," Adam's voice rose in decibels, proof that he had thoroughly lost his cool, which was a very rare occurrence.

In Gabriel's memory, such a thing had happened only once before, when a guy kicked down one of the side exit doors after he got fired. Gabriel had hoped never to witness something of the kind. *'Eh, well...'*

"Adam, listen to me. It's not about rescuing them off the mountain," Gabriel tried to regain the upper hand, but apparently, Adam's intentions didn't rhyme with his. The man refused to let him continue with explanations.

"But what's it about? They didn't fall off the train now, did they?" the man asked, and sharp sarcasm dripped off his tongue. "I'd have heard something on the news if something like that had happened," he drew the correct conclusion.

"It's worse than that," Gabriel interjected.

"What the heck could be worse than that?" Adam asked with exasperation now.

Gabriel breathed in deeply once more and took a mouthful of his hot coffee, burning his tongue. He shrugged, flexing his fist not to hiss loudly, and he let Adam's anger and exasperation wash over him.

"They're dead, all right," Gabriel snapped afterward. He didn't know how else to say it so he went for blunt.

"How the heck did they die?" Adam fairly roared, and his disbelief burnt through the phone line.

Gabriel rolled his eyes, even though his insides twisted. Anxiety had fisted around his heart, hampering his breathing.

"Someone killed them, Adam," Gabriel said in a deadpan tone of voice, annoyed with Adam's constant interruptions.

That way, they would have reached the conclusion of that conversation sometime next year, and Gabriel found that he didn't have the patience to go on. Heck, he didn't know if he had another year.

"Who killed them?" his manager's voice sounded a bit frayed at the edges, as if he tried to keep his shock under control but didn't quite manage to do it.

Gabriel knew that it was a lot to take in. No one would have expected such news when people left for a banal team building trip. If he hadn't been there at the scene of the crimes, he would have had a hard time to believe it either.

"I don't know. The police don't know either, although..."

"Although what?" Adam barked, apparently incapable to keep his mouth shut until he got all the details.

Gabriel scowled, eyeing the phone with distaste. "They're somewhat inclined to believe that I'm the murderer," Gabriel decided to go with full disclosure. Someone would have told Adam that sooner or later, anyway.

"Oh, man. Why would you have killed them? A team building trip is not a life and death matter. And who died by the way?"

"First we found Mia's body," Gabriel related, closing his eyes. He practically could hear the riot of Adam's thoughts at such a revelation.

A pause ensued, and Gabriel smirked, visualizing the little wheels turning inside Adam's head.

"I see," Adam said softly. "I don't have too much trouble seeing you kill that one," he nigh on whispered.

"Gee, thanks, Adam," Gabriel replied with sarcasm. "Don't forget to tell that to the police as well," he thought to add, as an indefinite feeling of frustration and vulnerability poked at his chest. "They might even dance a jig, happy to have more evidence piling up against me."

Disappointment in another human being wasn't something easy to swallow, and Gabriel had never expected Adam to sell him so short.

"Who else died?" Adam inquired, brushing off Gabriel's outburst as unimportant.

He didn't have any intention to express his personal beliefs in front of the police. In Adam's opinion, everyone had to do their job. Pointing fingers at his employees didn't fall under his job description.

"Alex," Gabriel replied dryly. Bitterness lingered on his tongue when he uttered the man's name. He still couldn't reconcile with Alex's pointless demise.

The man had never wronged anyone, quite the opposite. He had always helped as much as he could, and mostly at his own expense. A kinder man had never walked the earth. Now, he would never walk it again.

"I see. At least I can't see you murdering Alex," Adam said without hesitation.

"Thanks so much for your vote of confidence," Gabriel smirked, far from mollified.

"It is a vote of confidence," Adam didn't deny it. "Anyway, what's going on now? What are the police going to do?"

"The police are conducting an investigation, of course," Gabriel replied in a tired tone of voice. He rubbed the base of his nose between his fingers, feeling tired to the bones. "I was invited to move out of the villas, so the company isn't paying for my stay there anymore, so that you know," he had the mean pleasure to point out.

He had disliked Adam's earlier allegations immensely, and he felt better to pay him back. Adam tried to say something, but Gabriel wasn't going to allow any more interruptions.

"I had to invest in clothes as well, by the way. The police confiscated everything I had. Evidence, you know," he continued with derision.

"What about the others?" Adam inquired, glossing over Gabriel's words.

He couldn't care less about Gabriel's expenses right then. His employees fell like flies, and apparently no one could come up with any rational explanation.

"Probably, they're still there," Gabriel replied with a shrug. "I wouldn't know. I was advised to cease any communication with all of them, and that's what I did. I took their advice to heart," he shrugged, his sarcasm pouring along the line.

"But you're in charge of the team, man," Adam countered. "Even if the police say that you are out, you still need to make sure that our people are all right," he pointed out.

"Not anymore," Gabriel replied in a quiet tone of voice. "If you check your emails, Adam, you will find my resignation, and it's effective immediately. As I can't do my job anyway, I didn't think you'd expect any notice."

Gabriel wetted his mouth with some orange juice, turning his head to the left and gazing toward the ridges of the mountains. The landscape calmed his erratically beating heart and eased his weariness.

"I know it is a short notice, but I suppose it is for the best," he said like an afterthought when his boss failed to fill in the silence with something.

"I see," Adam whispered, disbelief echoing in his voice.

"Then all's good," Gabriel chirped with fake cheerfulness. "I will let you know if I find out something. If not me, then probably the police will contact you," he clarified.

"I will be waiting, and I will keep my phone with me at all times. This is not something we could sweep under the rug," Adam cautioned him and disconnected the call.

"As if I could have missed that," Gabriel glowered at the blinking screen, and with an irate gesture, he threw the cell phone on the table, picking up his cup of coffee again.

He brought it to his lips, but his gaze fell on Magda's graceful silhouette, and he didn't have a chance to sip from the still hot coffee. The young woman had just stepped out of the cottage and walked lazily toward him, the heel of her sandals clunking softly on the tiles.

CHAPTER NINE

The shock of seeing Magda jolted through Gabriel's body like lightning, turning him into a live wire. Electric shocks ran to all his extremities, making him twitch.

Startled, he sloshed the scolding liquid over the rim of the mug, and the instant sting shook him. Gabriel hissed in pain and then swore under his breath.

He couldn't understand why all those things kept happening to him lately. He understood bad karma and respected it, but that was way over the top already.

A man was entitled to a break, wasn't he? He needed one, and right then, but providence didn't seem in the mood to hand him one.

Those last few months had drained virtually all the strength and hope out of him, and his inane optimism simply couldn't keep up with every single whack over the head he took.

Gabriel hurried to pick up a napkin and dabbed at the wet burning spots on his skin even though it seemed a little too late for that. He scowled, looking at the back of his hand. He knew that the red angry blotches budding on his hand would turn into blisters long before the end of the day, so he cursed his lack of control over his own fate and motions once more.

He had seen beautiful women before. Some of them had been more beautiful than the young woman before his eyes. She might have seemed more intriguing than most, but that didn't mean he should turn into an idiot each and every time he laid his eyes on her.

Discreetly, he checked his white t-shirt for spills. Spotting the splatters on the once-upon-the-time pristine tee annoyed him, and he muttered with dismay. He had bought that shirt only the other day, and that was the first time he had worn it.

He patted at the tee with another napkin diligently, even though he didn't entertain any illusions that he would be able either to clean the shirt or play down his knee-jerk reaction at the sight of the young woman.

The inspector had certainly spied everything that happened. She had just come out of the small restaurant and her eyes had darted at him practically instantly.

Gabriel wondered if she had something like a radar system built inside her brain. Her gaze had found him without hesitation.

The man couldn't look away while she sauntered toward him, and he didn't fail to notice the inspector's steady gaze on his rushed gestures.

A naughty light twinkled in the hazel eyes that had never strayed off him, while a mute laughter curved those full lips he had been obsessing over ever since their first encounter. Every fiber in his body begged for a mere taste of her, even though he was aware that his thoughts shouldn't go there.

Her skin glowed under the morning sun, and she looked fresh and so damn young that his heart sang. He quelled the ditty out of his traitorous heart but couldn't take his gaze off her.

She seemed at home there on that tiled patio. Those surroundings, with the terrace lined with pots brimming with colorful and cheery flowers fitted her just fine.

Gabriel noticed her grin but couldn't argue against it. Anyone would have snickered at him. His teenager behavior hinted either at a sugar rush or the panic of bumping into his secret crush, the prettiest girl in the school, who wouldn't even bother to notice his existence.

"I thought I left that far, very far behind me," he muttered with irritation. "More fool I."

Gabriel ignored her smile and gave the woman a once-over, feeling pretty safe hiding his gaze behind the dark lenses of his sunglasses.

Magda's dark hair, gathered in a thick bouncing ponytail, drew his eyes. He wondered how it would have felt if he had run his fingers through it, and something tightened in his belly.

Feeling the blood rushing in his cheeks, he clenched his hand in a tight fist and tried to focus on something else. He needed the illusion of control.

The strap of a small functional bag hung over Magda's shoulder, and her fingers curled around it like an afterthought. Gabriel noticed a ridiculous pen clipped on the side of the bag, and his lips twitched with unconcealed humor. The woman did like her pens. She would always have one, either in her hand or somewhere close to the tips of her fingers.

A pair of worn-out jeans hugged the young woman's narrow hips, which swung gently with every step she took. Gabriel's pupils slightly dilated, and his tongue snaked out and lapped at his suddenly dry lips.

His gaze swept over Magda's small frame, clothed in a sunny yellow tee which fell to the top of her thighs. He stared at the deep V-neckline, satisfied that she was unaware that his eyes strayed to some choice spots on her body. He wouldn't have lived something like that down.

His eyes fell on the woman's bright yellow toenails encased in light white sandals, and warmth spread through his body, in spite of the cool morning breeze.

A moment later, Gabriel's forehead creased. Not long ago, he had promised himself not to let another woman get to him, and here he was, just a few days later, falling into the same stupid pattern.

"You never learn, you, stupid mutt," he muttered to himself, furious enough to drench both the stinging and his manly impulses with the waves of the flaming anger directed at his own person.

He threw the napkin back on the table and picked up his coffee cup again with a steady hand. This time, he brought it to his lips without any accidents, and practically drained it without feeling the burn of the liquid before Magda got to the table.

He didn't bother to stand up when she approached but waved at her to take a seat. She arched a brow, slightly annoyed with his blatant rudeness. A moment later, she shrugged, and choosing the chair across from him, she sat down.

They looked at each other for a couple of moments, and then Magda leaned over the table and pulled his sunglasses off his nose with a quick gesture.

"Hey, they're mine," he protested and launched over the table to grab them back, although the reaction made him flash back to grade school.

"Have I said differently?" she asked in a haughty tone of voice. "I merely removed them because I prefer to see the eyes of the people I'm talking to," she shrugged, leaning back in her chair.

"Maybe I don't want you to see my eyes," he replied in a huff, feeling petty and childish but unable to control his responses.

"Not a smart move if you want me not to think the worst of you," she shook her head, a grin in the corner of her mouth.

"You'll think anything you want anyway," he shrugged, but threw the sunglasses onto the table with a negligent motion.

"Of course, I will," she conceded with a nod. "It's my prerogative, after all," she said with obvious amusement. "You should put some butter on those burns," she pointed her chin toward the red blotches on his hand. "It won't blister that way," she informed him, nodding wisely.

"Really? Or are you just making fun of me?" Gabriel asked hesitantly, unsure if he should start slathering butter all over the back of his hand. It seemed weird.

"Why would I?" the woman raised a shoulder inquiringly. "It's not like I would have anything to gain by poking fun at you," she observed in an even tone of voice.

Gabriel stared at her through narrowed eyes for a few seconds, then grabbed the butter knife and started slathering the white goo liberally all over the abused skin. Relief came almost immediately, and he sighed with contentment.

"Are you hungry?" he inquired, pointing toward the platters on the table. "We can ask for a plate for you, you know."

He hadn't left too much food on the table but was sure that she still could have scraped a snack together.

Magda refused with a brief headshake but didn't look up at him. Her eyes followed his ministrations attentively.

"Maybe you'd like some coffee," he proposed expectantly, looking at her sideways and hoping that she would shift her attention somewhere else.

"A coffee would be good," she agreed. "I've already asked for some when I passed through the restaurant, so you don't have to worry about it," she informed him.

He just moved his shoulders to show that he didn't care one way or another. It was the same thing for him.

"By the way, I think you've spread enough butter on your hand now," she said with repressed laughter in her voice. "You can stop," she insisted when he ignored her words and continued piling the butter on his skin.

"Better more than less," he grumbled, and Magda shook her head.

"Not in this case, it's not," she retorted.

When she noticed his inquisitive gaze, her mien changed.

"Besides, you will see that in the end, it will hurt more," she added in a nonchalant tone of voice. "Your skin can soak in only so much grease. Then you'll have to wipe the excess off your hand, and that will cause some pain, believe me," she made a point in underlining the consequences.

Gabriel merely waved the hand with the butter knife dismissively, but then, he took a moment and reconsidered his actions. Magda grinned when he started muttering under his breath while scrutinizing the back of his hand as if he hadn't seen it before.

However, after a couple of seconds, she shook her head to clear it. She had no business to allow him to amuse her.

It wasn't a very good idea to find him cute either. Although she had bumped his name down on the suspects' list, he was still under investigation. There were too many things that had remained unanswered.

However, his bad boy attitude called to her at a primal level. She also couldn't shake the impression that in fact, his behavior concealed insecurity, and that seemed somewhat endearing, in total contrast with the hard-heartedness that often glimmered in his deep-set amber eyes and sometime showed in the hard line of his mouth.

"What?" Gabriel asked when he looked up at her and caught her watching him.

Magda shrugged her feelings and thoughts aside, as unimportant, and leaned back in her chair, looking for a more comfortable position. "I wanted to talk to you some more," she started saying, but the waitress chose that moment to bring fresh coffee.

Magda thanked her with a warm smile, and once the woman left, she busied herself with preparing a cup of coffee exactly as she liked it.

She stirred the sugar and milk in the hot potent brew and then shifted her eyes toward Gabriel, who was watching her with hawk-like eyes.

"Anything on your mind, Inspector?" he asked matter-of-factly, feeling that the discussion would shift toward unpleasant and serious issues.

He wanted to play it cool so that the Inspector didn't delve too deep in his inner thoughts, so he schooled his features not to show any sign of distress or curiosity.

Nonetheless, Magda sensed his wariness. The man stared at her without blinking, but then, his fingers flexed on the knife handle, betraying his dread.

She couldn't blame him anyway. She didn't imagine that anyone would take a possible indictment for a double crime without qualms. Even one crime would have bothered him.

"We talked to your people yesterday," she informed him in a dry tone of voice, her gaze steady on him.

Magda waved her hand, trying to diminish the importance of her words. She intended to let him believe whatever he wanted to.

She had learned that most of the time, it was better not to lead the culprits or witnesses when you were looking for answers. It helped a lot with getting worthwhile responses.

"Anyway, I was thinking to check some of the things with you," she went on, watching him intently. "You know your people better than I," she shrugged.

Gabriel still didn't show any outward reaction at her words. He merely looked at her, mildly interested just because she was talking to him, and it wouldn't have been polite not to listen.

Bothered because he didn't do anything else but arch his brows with something close to a moderate interest in her words, Magda began drumming her fingers on the rim of the coffee cup.

The man was good enough at hiding what he was thinking. She had to give him that, but that didn't mean that she had to like it.

"I'm talking about impressions, facts...," she moved her hands widely. "You know, Gabriel, the usual," she added, lifting a dainty peachy shoulder.

Gabriel's eyes followed the motion hungrily, the man forgetting about his disinterested behavior for one moment. Luckily, part of his brain still worked, and Gabriel frowned.

"Could you be more specific? I can assure you that this is the first time I've found myself in such a situation," he replied with sarcasm.

She narrowed her eyes slightly, sipped from her coffee, and then lifted that one brow that irked him.

"I haven't made a habit of getting involved in a crime every other day, you know," he continued glibly, and irony shone in his eyes.

Magda drew a deep breath and shook her head. She returned his ironic gaze, and the corners of her mouth turned up, although she didn't feel very charitable right that moment.

"I'm trying to help you here, Gabriel, so there's no need to..."

"Huh," Gabriel interrupted her offensively. "Don't try to sell me on that damn old thing, Inspector," he barked.

His eyes flashed at her with smoldering defiance, and the man hardly refrained himself from thumping his hand on the table. He was sick and tired to be the bottom of everyone's jokes.

Gabriel didn't have any illusions. He assumed that he had a certain idea how things worked in Magda's field. An inspector would use anything to make a suspect talk, and Gabriel didn't feel like falling into that trap.

"Look here, Inspector. First of all, you're trying to help yourself and reach your performance expectations," he waved the hand with the knife between the two of them.

Magda's forehead wrinkled and she took a moment to calm down. It hurt to know that she wanted to help him, and he merely threw her kindness back into her face.

"Would you be careful with that knife, Gabriel?" she requested in a harder tone of voice that she had wanted. "Someone might take that gesture of yours as a threat," she looked at him meaningfully.

She clasped her hands together in her lap, careful that the tablecloth hid them from his eyes. Magda had never liked to threaten people. She didn't have it in her, and the words he had forced her to utter didn't sit very well with her either.

Gabriel threw the knife on his plate at once and winced when it clinked loudly. He looked straight into Magda's eyes and said, "I'm not threatening you, of course. It would have been plain stupid, don't you think?" he cocked his head to the right.

The man studied her immobile features attentively but couldn't read her.

"It just happened," he stressed out. "I've purely forgotten that I was holding the knife. I didn't mean anything by that," he opened his arms widely to prove that he didn't have any bad intentions.

They studied each other warily for a few moments, and Gabriel breathed deeply. He needed to get a handle on the situation and soon. He knew that it wouldn't help him at all to upset her, even though he had to say what was on his mind.

"I've already dealt with the first point of my argument. Let's get to the second. You're probably trying to catch a murderer, I know that and I want very much that you succeed. But don't try to convince me that you care about what would happen to me in the process," he forgot about handling things with care, and anger slashed through his words and flashed in his pupils.

"You're a very cynical man, Gabriel, I have to say," Magda pursed her lips in disappointment.

She watched him for a few seconds more, and only after she pondered her words carefully, she continued.

"Still, I do care about you somewhat. I mean, like about any other human being," she rushed to add so that he wouldn't misunderstand her and draw any wrong conclusions. "Doing my job or closing a case isn't everything. I need to make sure that I have the right person in custody," she chided him, her reproachful gaze cutting through him.

"One thing is clear. You're very dedicated," he shook his head. "It's Sunday, after all."

Magda smiled warily at him and shrugged. She picked up her cup and sipped, however her eyes never left his face.

"You're not from around here," she replied softly afterward. "I think you'd like to go back home and not spend money on a room and food in this town for longer than necessary," she waved her hand, encompassing the surrounding area. "I don't mind working on a Sunday. I can take a few days off when I finish this investigation."

"Very thoughtful of you," Gabriel grumbled, pissed off with himself because he let her words impress him. He didn't want to be impressed or look for redeeming qualities in the woman before his eyes. She was the enemy right then, at least until she found the real killer and backed off. "What do you need from me?" he asked reluctantly, understanding that in spite of everything he had to give her something in return.

"Your opinions about your team," Magda pointed out.

An ugly laugh rolled off Gabriel's lips, and a rose hue powdered the top of his cheekbones.

"What's so funny?" the woman inquired, although she doubted that the man found anything entertaining right then.

Gabriel waved his fingers while looking for the correct turn of phrase. He shook his head a couple of times, and then decided to enlighten her.

"I resigned my position last night. My job, to be correct."

"Why?" Magda's eyes widened. She hadn't expected anything as radical as that.

"Because I couldn't do the job anymore," he confessed.

"But the investigation will end, and probably soon. It isn't like it would last a lifetime," she contradicted him.

"It wasn't just the investigation," he replied in a weary tone of voice.

"What else then?" she asked nonplussed, and her bafflement touched him, which he resented immediately.

"I already told you when we spoke yesterday," he snapped, unwilling to humiliate himself once more. "I told you that my team doesn't respect my position anymore, and my authority is shot."

"Yes, you said something like that," she nodded. "However, things can't be so bad," she continued, in a steady tone of voice.

"Allow me to know better," he barked, and to hide his rising emotions, he plucked a strip of bacon off the platter and popped it into his mouth.

Magda's lips twitched, and she cleared her throat. "I would allow you that, but you see, I spoke to your people almost all day yesterday," she pointed out.

"So that would make you an expert?" he retorted with annoyance, aware that he was getting close to be gallingly rude again.

"No, not an expert, no," she shook her head, folding her hands on the table.

Magda assessed him with a clinical eye, and her opinion of him didn't suffer any radical changes. "But," she stressed out, "aside from a few people that would have bitched about anyone and at any given time, not only you specifically, the others seemed to appreciate you, even though, true enough, some of them displayed some temporary disappointment in you."

"Yeah, the story of my life," he made an attempt at levity and wiggled his brows.

"Might be," she shrugged. "However, you should consider that their disappointment appears to be temporary. They still believe that you will steer things in the right direction."

Gabriel shifted his gaze toward the highlands where the calcareous rocks glistened in the light of the summer sun. He breathed deeply and then turned back to Magda.

The woman sipped her coffee unhurriedly, and her moist lips triggered an unusual response in his belly.

"Then they'll have to go on being disappointed. I for one don't have anything more to give," he stated without emotion, determined to ignore the woman's effect on his body or mind.

"I think that's a pity, but that's just my opinion. You have to make your choices," Magda shrugged.

"That's exactly, my opinion, Inspector. Meanwhile, why don't you run by me those questions you have?"

CHAPTER TEN

"So Andy and Alex were very good friends, I gather," Magda jotted a brief note in her notebook.

"I don't think that there was anyone who didn't like Alex," Gabriel replied pensively, rolling his cigarette between his fingers. "He... knew to listen and help..." he added as an afterthought, while his gaze shifted from Magda to the mountains.

Unshed tears shone in the man's eyes, and the lines around his mouth deepened. Looking at him, Magda understood that Gabriel's feelings for Alex ran deep. He wasn't a good enough actor to blindside her.

"For how long did he work with you?" she asked softly, and with an iron fist, she squashed the impulse to lay her hand on his.

That would have been a lot of shades of wrong. She couldn't afford to offer any consolation to a presumptive suspect, even if her instincts screamed that he hadn't been the one to dole out those cruel punishments.

"Since the beginning," Gabriel turned to her. "We actually started with the project. The guinea pigs, if you want," he chuckled without any trace of cheer. "Not quite a year down the road, I broke the mold and tried for the supervisor position... The rest is history," he lifted a shoulder and erased any expression off his face, giving Magda the sensation that he was closing a window on his thoughts and feelings.

"Did you have any... problems with him?" she probed further.

He shook his head, squeezed his eyes for a couple of seconds, and then replied, "No, I don't think so... Well, I know he was upset with my... let's say, lack of commitment or maybe involvement in the team... Otherwise, I don't think so," he gave another shake of his head.

"That's what most of your people said," she observed. "With two exceptions," she amended her statement.

Gabriel looked at her for a few long seconds, and his unblinking stare poked at her, making her feel out of place. Without taking his eyes off hers, the man lit his roll-up with careful and measured gestures, and only afterward, his eyes darted somewhere above her head.

"I don't really care about what they have to say about me," he noted in a hard tone of voice. "I don't want validation for my actions," he shook his head a couple of times. "Well, not anymore."

Magda studied his expression and bowed her lips slightly.

"You're disappointed," she observed, the words out of her mouth before she realized it.

Gabriel ignored the inner jolt that shot through him, and his forehead furrowed.

"In what?" he asked with derision, a sudden urge to wipe off her grin and bring her self-assurance down a notch.

He had noticed that the woman was able to point to some things with astute accuracy, and he loathed that. He didn't need anyone else to commiserate with him, and he disliked people who could read him with close to no effort. His thoughts and feelings belonged to him, and it was no one's business to stick their nose in.

Magda took her time to reply to him. First, she folded her narrow hands neatly before her on the top of the table, calling his attention to her somewhat nervous fingers.

She had a good idea what his reaction would be at her answer, and she was just buying some time. If she had kept her mouth shut and stuck with the facts, they wouldn't have reached the point where they had to tiptoe around feelings.

"You're disappointed in yourself," she said in the end because it was of no use to avoid the answer.

Gabriel's eyes blazed with shame and fury at the same time. His fingers tightened around the cigarette, snapping it in two, and he got singed once more.

His nostrils flared, and he spit out such an ugly string of dirty words that Magda merely gaped at him, her eyes going round in shock.

She had heard others indulging in a good session of swearing. In her profession it would have been impossible not to. Still, in her experience, no one had ever reached Gabriel's level of proficiency in the field.

The man stopped his litany of crude words with a click of his teeth. Getting a hold of his temper, he looked at Magda sideways. His cheeks had turned reddish and burnt with anger, shame and embarrassment at the same time.

"Not a word," he growled when she opened her mouth to say something.

She snapped her mouth shut and nibbled at her lower lip to keep her amusement in check. Sometimes men's egos were fragile things and needed soothing.

Gabriel had shocked her for a moment with his extensive knowledge of the cussing terminology, as well as with his passion in uttering those words.

However, he also entertained her with his behavior, and more than she would have expected.

"If you insist, I can apologize for my gutter vocabulary, but other than that, I wouldn't welcome anything else coming from you right now," he insisted and then turned his attention to the pulsing aches the new burn had caused.

"Not even some advice?" Magda asked with badly suppressed cheer.

Gabriel simply snarled at her, and his amber eyes narrowed to slits.

"Look here, you're the police, I get it. But that doesn't give you carte blanche to torment me and make fun of my mishaps," he thundered, punctuating his statement with a slap of his undamaged hand on the table.

The dishes clattered, and he dashed a quick gaze toward them to see if he had damaged anything. That was the last thing he needed right then.

Magda grinned slyly at him, and then shook her head. "Gabriel, you'd like to keep everything in very neat pockets, but that doesn't work all the time. You'd also prefer that people don't take a look at what you think or feel, and that doesn't work either, you know, especially if you're involved in a criminal investigation."

"This wasn't about the investigation," he retorted, and the lines around his mouth deepened even more because of the pain and his sense of inability to find a way out of the maze his life had turned into.

"I wasn't talking about the investigation, either," the woman pointed out. "Anyway, my advice is the same as before. Put some butter on that burn, and you will feel better," she pointed her chin to the butter dish on the table.

"I don't need to be babied, you know," he barked, while he grabbed the knife to spread the butter on his skin.

"All of us need babying now and then," she replied with a laugh. "Even big bad boys like you," she continued, a twinkle in her eyes.

"You see, I was right," he threw the knife back on the table. "Making fun of me," he concluded.

Magda assessed his mien and lifted her right brow.

"Should I understand you don't think that you are a big bad boy?" she inquired with bafflement.

"Look here, I'm not a boy," he replied hotly.

"That I noticed," she nodded. "It's only an expression. If you prefer I'd say a big bad man, it isn't a problem for me. I can adjust," she lifted one of her dainty peachy shoulders.

"I know I'm not so big," Gabriel replied leaning back in his chair. He decided that he had made a fool of himself enough so he had to turn it down for a while.

"Not from where I stand," Magda contradicted him. "I haven't said you were a giant, have I? But big... Yes, that you are," she repeated, giving him a once over furtively.

"All right, what's the angle you're working now?" Gabriel leaned forward, his eyes hard and unblinking.

Magda studied him for a few seconds. Her brows furrowed in concentration, but she didn't reach any conclusion.

"What exactly do you mean?" she inquired with puzzlement.

"You know very well what I'm talking about," he didn't give up. "You're flattering me now. That does mean that you want something from me. What do you want?" he asked bluntly, unwilling to let her action slide.

Magda's eyes went round, and she tilted her head to the right, watching him as if he had been an unknown specimen of a recently discovered species.

"You have a problem not only with trust but also with self-confidence," she concluded. "You should work on that," she said, standing up and grabbing her shoulder bag from the back of the chair where she had hung it when she arrived. "When a woman tells you that you're a big bad boy, you smile and maybe say *thank you*. You don't turn into an asshole and prove to all and sundry that you don't give a rat's ass about yourself. I don't need to flatter you in order to discover the facts I need to conclude my investigation, Gabriel. Unfortunately, you have proved to me right now that t Mia did do a serious number on you. Well, so that you know, that gives you more than probable cause for killing her," she said matter-of-factly and turned on her heels, striding with quick and angry steps toward the French doors leading onto the patio.

"Just a damn second,

Gabriel crossly pushed his chair back and jumped up.

"I don't have a second to waste on someone who reacts as stupidly as you," Magda replied without turning her head and then disappeared inside the B & B.

Gabriel had started after her but stopped, her words stabbing him right in the middle of his chest. He flopped back into his chair and picked up his coffee cup to wet his mouth and got nothing.

He peeked inside the cup and scowled. It was empty. He put it back on the table and stretched to grab Magda's. Peering in her cup brought a grin on his lips. The inspector had left half the coffee in the mug. With a shrug, Gabriel drained it at once and grimaced afterward. He drank black coffee. Magda seemed to favor something like milk and sugar with a hint of coffee.

CHAPTER ELEVEN

"I'm inclined to believe that the killer is that Gabriel Barna," Stefan insisted with inflexibility, and the other inspectors and forensic technicians watched him with curiosity, which wasn't something new.

Magda looked at him sideways. Stefan was a good investigator on his good days, but those were very far and in between.

Worse yet, he didn't have too much of an imagination. He counted on the obvious, but not always what seemed obvious showed to an inspector the true when it came to apprehending a murderer.

"I understand," Magda replied softly. "And we'll be looking into that, of course," she nodded to appease him.

"Are you sure that you're willing to look in that direction?" Stefan asked dryly, and a scowl marred his face.

"What do you mean, Stefan?" Magda asked quietly, and the other people in the room averted their eyes.

Everyone had caught the gist of the man's words, but no one was prepared to let him notice what they thought about him.

"You know very well what I am talking about," he replied boldly, waving his hand contemptuously. "I saw how you look at him. You like that guy. Of course, you don't want him to be guilty. But he is," he pointed his thick forefinger to her. "I'll eat my cap if he isn't," he thumped his fisted hand on the conference table.

"I see. Well, I am sure that everyone knows me better than that," Magda replied flatly, thinking that she would make sure that the man ate his cap.

The expressions on the other people in the conference room proved that they would have liked to have front row seats when something like that happened.

"If he's the killer, he'll go down... Even if I might like him, as you say," she replied with disdain, her eyes piercing Stefan with disparagement.

It was no secret that there was some bad blood between the inspector and the chief inspector, and all the bad blood was on Stefan's side. Magda didn't really care about his pettiness or his dreams of grandeur, even though she knew what the man believed.

Stefan hadn't made a secret of his opinions about how Magda had become a Chief Inspector instead of him. He had stated several times that the reason she got where she was had nothing to do with her ability to do her job.

He was sure that he would have made a finer Chief than Magda. He would have solved cases faster without dragging his feet as Magda used to do.

When evidence shone in your face, you had to accept it. Tiptoeing around it didn't amount to anything in the end.

Nevertheless, the others didn't share his high opinion about his skills. He knew that too. Some had even wondered openly if he wouldn't have been a better fit for another type of job within the police force, and that had cut deeply into his pride.

As a matter of fact, everybody considered that he was good at gathering evidence but not so good at interpreting the clues. He never looked farther than what lay under his nose, and a lot of people thanked God almost daily that he hadn't made the grade. Not just a few people who had had the bad luck to fall under his investigations cursed him till the kingdom come.

All the techs and the inspectors believed that Magda had been the best choice for that position in spite of her being a woman, and a young one at that. Yes, she might have had emotions, but never on the job. She was a true professional and treated all her investigations with careful attention.

She was good at gathering evidence and making ittalk to her. She never stopped digging until she was sure that when she arrested someone, that someone was the right person.

Magda used to say that some mistakes were unavoidable, but most of them weren't, so it depended on her not to send someone to prison if that person wasn't the culprit. Her duty was only to look carefully at all the pieces before her eyes and build the jigsaw puzzle from scratch. Until all the pieces fit, her job wasn't done.

"I doubt he could be," the forensic team leader's low rumble broke the awkward silence that filled the room.

A man well in his fifties, with a gray beard as the focal point on his face, he didn't give a fig about office politics. His interest lay only in the evidence he processed. Some of his younger trainees called him *Pops*, and the others knew him as Titi.

As he hadn't ever had a note on his personal file for mishandling evidence, not many dared to contradict him when he spoke. Almost no one thought of that, though.

Stefan turned his bleak eyes in the man's direction. His gaze narrowed, and two spots of red painted the top of his cheekbones. He had never liked Titi. The man had pointed to one or another of Stefan's mistakes too many times.

"What do you mean?" he asked in a hoarse voice.

"We analyzed the splatters," the man explained.

"Splatters tell you jack about who committed the crime," Stefan scowled, an ugly grin widening on his lips.

"Well, they don't leave a business card with the name of the murderer, that's true," the forensic expert agreed with a drawl. "But we don't really need that to learn something from the splatters," he said wisely.

The man moved his shoulders to work out the kinks in them. He had been already hunching over photographs since six a.m. and his body complained.

However, he knew that such meetings always brought a sort of a whining from Stefan, and Titi was determined not to let the prig win anything if he got into an argument with Magda. So he had worked harder and longer to make that happen.

The grapevine had it that Stefan had pointed out that Magda was being spellbound by one of the suspects. Titi didn't doubt that Stefan would try to bank on that allegation and make the woman look bad. So the forensic expert had toiled hard to have something to help with her defense.

"And what have you learned?" Stefan growled, at the same time waving a hand with derision toward the forensic team. He didn't consider that they had earned a place at the conference table, and he had made his opinion known several times in the past. Their place was at the bottom of the food chain.

"First, you should know that the guy found in the room upstairs wasn't killed there," Titi said, looking at the coroner, who approved his words with a few nods.

"No one told me that," Stefan interjected, taking it personally that no one had bothered enough to let him know something as important as that.

"Well, son, you took the last day and a half off, you know," Titi opened his arms to show that no one else was guilty for the man's lack of knowledge.

"It was a weekend," Stefan replied through tightened teeth. "People don't work over the weekend," he pointed out.

"Some do," the coroner replied in a tone of voice that didn't broach any argument.

Lucian Cassian, the coroner, had acquired a certain fame in the police, and few dared not to listen to him. With over twenty-five years under his belt as the county's coroner, his experience spoke for itself.

At the man's words, Stefan gritted his teeth and pierced Magda with an angry gaze. He just knew that she was the one who put him in that situation.

The coroner shook his head noticing the man's viperous stare, and then continued, "Magda made a good point in explaining that all the suspects didn't live here in town, and we couldn't hold them here indefinitely. We couldn't have asked them to pay from their pockets for their living expenses until we could do our job nicely, from nine to five during the week," he added mockingly.

"It's not our business to make the suspects feel good," Stefan muttered, but his eyes failed to meet the doctor's.

"But it is our job not to hold suspicion over everyone and make everyone uncomfortable if we could do it differently," Magda replied quietly.

"Police work is not for the softhearted," Stefan replied with anger and scorn in his voice.

"Police work is for the fair," Lucian Cassian cut the argument short.

The coroner's reply made Stefan black gaze dart to him covertly, but the man merely shrugged noticing the inspector's gesture.

"Anyway, because you were complaining that you didn't know all the facts, let me enlighten you. I could do that faster if we stop theorizing upon the essence of police work and return to the subject in hand," the doctor pinned the inspector with a hard stare.

Stefan flipped his hand as if inviting the doctor to continue, and Lucian shook his head. The inspector never ceased to impress him in a negative way.

"The man wasn't killed in that room upstairs," he started explaining in clipped words. "He was murdered in the same room with the girl, and after he died someone carried him in that bedroom."

"Which doesn't exonerate that Barna," Stefan said with glee in his voice.

"No, that doesn't," the coroner admitted. "However, the splatters Titi was talking about prove beyond any doubt that the two crimes happened at the same time. Considering the evidence, we can safely conclude that the man entered the room when the woman was beaten to death. Probably he tried to intervene," Cassian alleged.

"He definitely tried to intervene," Magda contributed to the picture of the crime. "From what I learned about the guy, he wouldn't have stepped back when a woman was beaten, even if he didn't like that woman."

"You purely extrapolate," Stefan rushed to say. "That's what you always do, even though it's just wishful thinking," he said reproachfully, shaking his head at her.

"From what I remember," a pixie-like blond, twenty-something woman chirped in, "Magda's always been right, even when she extrapolated."

Stefan narrowed his eyes to slits and pursed his lips before retorting, "You're a woman, Celia. It's no wonder you think like her."

"But I'm a man," a lanky guy around thirty said in a cool tone of voice. "And I agree with her assessment."

"I'm starting to feel the odd one out here," Stefan looked around the people gathered around the conference table, reserving an especially poisonous gaze for the lanky guy, Inspector Bogdan Damian.

"I'm sure that's not our fault," Cassian replied casually. "Apparently, we all think alike. You don't. You are indeed the odd one out. Maybe you should wonder why," he advised the younger man without malice.

Stefan clasped his hands on the table and gritted his teeth, ready to give a spicy reply to the coroner, regardless of the man status in the police. Celia leaned toward the inspector and laid her hand over his.

"I think you should listen to everything first, Stefan, and then make an opinion. You can't make a good analysis without having all the facts," she explained to him, patting the back of one of his hands.

Decisively, Stefan pulled his hands from underneath her palm and leaned back in his chair. "All right, continue," he invited the coroner.

At the same time, he tried to ignore Celia's sadness at his callous behavior. He hadn't invited her to offer him solace, so he didn't have to care about her hurt feelings. He had had enough of feelings since Magda took the Chief Inspector position, quite enough to last him for a lifetime.

"I did the post-mortem and then crossed-referenced my findings with the ones gathered by Titi's team," Lucian began.

He pulled a file closer to him and browsed through it. He took a couple of photos out of it and threw them in the middle of the table, closer to Stefan's place.

"It seems clear that at least two perpetrators were involved. We reconstructed the crimes and concluded that the killers started with beating the woman," he said, and looked around to see what the others were thinking. "There was even an attempt to rape her, if I consider the telling signs."

The forensic team murmured their agreement, and Celia and Bogdan nodded. Lucian gazed over at Stefan, but the inspector was looking at the photos and didn't return his gaze.

"While they kicked the woman around, the man came in, and as I said, he probably made a move to intervene," the doctor explained.

"We analyzed the blood splatter on the man's pants and shirt," one of the forensic experts continued. "We found some blood splatter from Mia, covered then with his blood. The evidence shows that he got hit from two sides with two different blunt objects," the man mentioned.

"Which we found in the living room downstairs," Titi intervened.

"Anyway, one of them moved Alex's body upstairs, while the other continued to hit Mia," Magda chimed in.

"How do you know that?" Stefan asked with sarcasm.

"Simple, son," Titi replied with a grin. "If the body was left in the living room until the woman expired, we would have found more of her blood on the man's body. As it wasn't, we found only a few spots, covered with his blood. Then, he was taken away."

"However, someone still punched the woman, because we found blood where the man's cadaver should have been," Damian contributed to the explanation.

"How the heck could you know where the body should have been?" Stefan asked with exasperation. "You're not a fortune teller."

"No, I'm not, but we found the spot where the man fell after he had been knocked over the head from two sides," Bogdan replied.

"We took samples of the blood on the carpet where his head hit down. Mia's blood splashed over his. It couldn't have if his body was still lying there," Titi shrugged.

"Then why didn't the woman run away while they were busy with the man?" Stefan asked, unwilling to surrender too easily.

"I think she tried," Magda replied softly. "She made it even to the door but someone caught her from behind. That someone banged her head onto the jamb. Titi found the traces there," she shifted her eyes toward the expert, and the man nodded sagely.

"That someone continued to hit the woman, while someone else draped the man's body over his shoulder to carry it up the stairs," Titi took up the running. "The person with the girl was just hitting her when the person carrying Alex passed by in his way out of the room. We found the woman's blood in a spot where it couldn't have reached otherwise. However, the position of Alex's body over the killer's shoulder explains how it landed there," Titi concluded.

"So we can draw the conclusion that we have to deal with at least two killers," Bogdan tapped his forefinger on the table.

Celia approved of his inference and added, "And one clearly is a man. I don't think there's a woman in that group capable to carry a man like Alex over her shoulder all the way up to that bedroom."

"I saw the girls in the group," Lucian intervened. "I also verified the strength necessary to inflict the damage to the two bodies," he continued looking from one person to another around the conference room. "I can safely declare that no woman in that group would have been one of the murderers," he shook his head with conviction. "It might be only if one of them is extremely insane, and her insanity gives her more strength than what we can notice with the naked eye," he added, but some doubt sneaked in his voice. "However, I can't buy that," he gave his head a resolute shake. "That would mean to extrapolate the heck out of it," he grinned.

"So we have two killers at least," Magda concluded. "Both are men, and both are able to inflict maximum damage to a strong guy with a few knocks."

"What about Mia?" Stefan wondered. "Her beating was different."

"That was, indeed," Magda agreed. "It was methodical and full of hatred. She was the intended victim. The man was only collateral damage."

No one said anything for a full minute, thinking about what had been revealed there and drawing their own conclusion.

Bogdan looked like he would have liked to add something but hadn't made up his mind to talk yet.

"What is it, Bogdan?" Magda asked.

The man hesitated a few moments, brushed the lock that had fallen over his forehead, and only after a few seconds, he spoke.

"From all those interviews, I understand that no one in the group liked Mia. She was conceited and selfish. She mocked every one and teased the guys something awful."

"Yes," Celia interjected. "That's what I gathered as well."

"So we have a motive for that crime. But I'm thinking..."

"What could you be thinking?" Stefan asked with unconcealed spite.

Bogdan merely lifted a brow, and then he turned to Magda. "What if we have a two-pronged motive here?"

Magda perked up in her chair and looked at him pensively.

"Interesting thinking," the Chief Inspector murmured.

"Yeah, maybe we have the spies of the century in our back yard," Stefan scoffed. However, he didn't like the looks he could notice on other people's faces.

Interest gleamed in Lucian Cassian's face, and Celia practically quivered with impatience to hear what Bogdan had to say.

"Let the boy talk," Titi intervened, slapping his hand on the table.

Stefan retreated in his shell, and his face darkened. He didn't see what Damian could bring to the table, but he noted that all the others mirrored Titi's thoughts.

"I was in on some of those interviews," Bogdan began his explanations. "From what I gathered, the guys are very angry with Gabriel Barna. That's a common denominator."

"Yes, that's true," Magda nodded. "I understand that things haven't been going well in that team for some time. The entire team considers that Barna is at the heart of the problems."

"Still, from what I heard, only some of them went along with the hypothesis that he killed those two people. The others didn't even want to hear about it."

"Yes, some even softened up toward him once they got the idea that we were looking in his direction," Celia commented.

"Exactly," Bogdan concurred. "However, I've noticed three or four who really hate the guy. Now, I'm thinking..." he murmured pensively.

The inspector's tone was so catchy that Celia and some of the forensic team leaned forward. Their action brought a smile on Magda's lips, and she shook her head with amusement.

"What if the killers wanted to get rid of the woman, to punish her, but at the same time to put everything on him?" Bogdan inquired, probing his colleagues' opinions.

"You might have something there," Lucian murmured. "It is possible, you know. Otherwise, why did they move Alex to his room?"

"Plus it is always good to have a patsy," Titi confirmed. "They needed someone to take the blame, didn't they?"

"So we should be looking to the people who hate him the most," Celia proposed.

"I think you're already in fairy-land right now," Stefan intervened in an acidic tone of voice.

He looked around the table with narrowed, grim eyes. He noticed the disbelief on the other people's faces and winced inwardly. Nevertheless, he decided to continue presenting his opinion.

"Things are always simpler. The guy hated the woman. Alex found him killing her, and Gabriel reacted. He's the killer," he slapped his palm over the edge of the table. "We should just arrest him."

The coroner shook his head as if he couldn't believe his ears. "Based on what evidence, I'd like to know," he inquired in a hard tone of voice.

"There were spots of blood on his jeans," the inspector put in with obstinacy.

"On the hem of his jeans which can be explained by his sleeping on that sofa that night," Titi intervened. "We cannot bend the evidence to support your theory, inspector," he continued. "A defense lawyer on his first day in court would be able to point out the weakness of such a case."

"No," Magda intervened. "We cannot arrest him. We need to look at the others," she pointed out.

"Because you have the hots for him?" Stefan asked, and his voice sounded full of malice.

Once, before she became a Chief Inspector and his boss, he had tried his hand at courting Magda, but she had refused him. He couldn't forgive that and never missed his chance to attack her.

"That's a... quite colorful expression," Magda said, looking Stefan straight in his eyes.

Her direct gaze, brimming with authority, hit him squarely in his chest, and he didn't enjoy it at all.

However, he didn't bend and didn't think of presenting an apology to the woman, although everyone looked at him with distaste.

He said it as he saw it. They didn't like it and that was their business, but that didn't mean he had to keep his mouth shut.

"I don't think I have the hots for him, as you put it so nicely. Nonetheless, I do like him, and probably, once this investigation ends, I might think about him now and then," Magda admitted.

She leaned further over the conference table and gazed intensely in Stefan's eyes. The man didn't even blink. He just stared at her with narrowed eyes.

"That doesn't mean that I won't arrest the real murderer, and if it turns out he is the one, he'll go behind bars," Magda continued. "I just like doing it by the book. I like to have my arrests supported by facts and evidence, not by narrow-mindedness," she stressed out.

"What the heck do you want to say by that?" clouds gathered in Stefan's eyes.

"Exactly what you've heard," Cassian intervened. "I'm pretty sure everyone agrees with Magda on this point, especially regarding you."

The doctor had had enough of the younger man's attitude. Lately, meetings of that kind lasted much longer because of him, and everyone had other things to do.

"I think you should ask for a transfer somewhere else, Stefan," he continued matter-of-factly. "It is very clear you can't accept Magda's leadership. It's like a thorn in your side, man," the doctor noted. "And the point is that she makes a good Chief Inspector. You can't stand that, so you'd better go," he concluded.

Stefan paled, and his fingers flinched on the table. The man leaned back in his chair and crossed his arms over his chest to hide his hands.

"It isn't the first time you've done your best to undermine an investigation and fray everyone's nerves with your pettiness," Lucian shook his head. "If you don't ask for a transfer, I will do it for you," he ended his tirade in a very hard tone of voice. "You might be a good inspector. The problem is that you don't use your skills here because you're too busy to take potshots at Magda."

"I don't need your advice," the inspector barely managed to push through his tight lips. Shame simmered in his chest, and his sight blurred.

"It's not only Lucian's advice, son," Titi decided to bring his input to the table. "It's everyone's. You should listen and do something worthwhile for you and your future. You're wasting your time here. Worse, you're wasting everyone else's," the older man shook his head with regret.

Stefan looked around at his colleagues' faces. The truth was neatly written there, so he stood up and left the conference room. Although he had told himself to show them that he was the bigger man, he couldn't refrain from slamming the door behind him.

CHAPTER TWELVE

Gabriel wandered through the small mountain town taking in the sights. He didn't have anything else to do with his time so he just moved around.

Well, he should have looked for a new job, but he didn't see the point for that right then. He had no idea how long he would be free to meander around so looking for a job seemed pointless. Better to hit the streets, roam the mountain trails. As long as he was free and could do that.

He wasn't sure how long his savings would last either, but whenever that thought popped into his head, he just ignored the issue. If you didn't think of a problem, then it didn't exist.

Gabriel had always been a bit of an optimist. He wouldn't have survived bullying in school otherwise, and he wouldn't pop back up after every time a woman let him down with a bang.

He had let himself forget that along the last few months, but he got back on track now. He might not hold a lot of hope about his future, but the present worked just fine. He had just to keep strolling around and charge his batteries. The weather was on his side, at least.

He had known for some time now that he needed to change the scenery and the job. He got pushed into doing it, and that was just fine. Now and then, he needed a nudge to do the right thing. He tended to procrastinate.

Moreover, he was satisfied that his team wouldn't suffer even though they had to remain in that town.

Before leaving the team, he had talked with Andy and handed him the money for their trip. The chat had been full of recriminations and potshots, but at least Gabriel knew that his people would have money to pay for their food without worrying that they didn't have enough dough with them or in their bank account.

On Tuesday, Adam called again and dazzled him, making him respect his former boss even more. Gabriel hadn't expected any kind of help from Adam. He had been convinced that the man would always chase the bottom line and profit so he would wash his hands off Gabriel.

Nonetheless, Adam had taken it upon him to speak to the police and see how things were. Afterward he had arranged to have money sent there so that the entire team could pay for their lodging and food.

The money had come directly to Gabriel, so he had had to contact the police and arrange for an escort to go to the B & B where the team landed, and pass the money on to Andy.

He had hoped to see Magda again, but he had been forced to content himself with the company of another young female inspector, Celia, and that of the grim inspector Stefan, who loathed Gabriel's guts.

Gabriel shuddered whenever he remembered the two hours he had spent in their company. The woman had been all right, but Stefan had treated him as if he were scum.

That man reminded him of one of the bullies he had encountered during his first years in school when he was too puny, shy and untrained to fight back. Well, he couldn't very well fight this one either. The inspector would have his ass thrown in jail in under two minutes.

Gabriel shook the inspector's image off his mind and shoved his hands in his pants pockets. He breathed in the mountain air deeply, scented with pine and fir, and continued his stroll, turning his steps onto a narrow, winding lane, leading to the outskirts of the town.

His thoughts returned to Adam. His soon-to-be-former manager had even argued with the financial department and obtained money to also cover Gabriel's expenses for the whole haul of nine days.

Adam accepted Gabriel's resignation but with a seven-day notice, thus making it as Gabriel had still been one of the company's employees and in conclusion on their payroll.

So Adam had forced the firm to cover for Gabriel's lodging and meals during those days. He had persuaded them that Gabriel was in that town because management had sent him there on a business, not because the man had wanted to have a few days of fun in the mountains. Therefore, the company also had to pay for the previous Saturday and Sunday, as it hadn't been Gabriel's choice to move out of the villa.

Gabriel took the road to the right when he got to a fork in the lane. He didn't break his stride although the slope became steeper. He was busy calculating that he had three more days with everything paid by his temporary employer. Afterward, it would be up to him and his meager savings.

He wiped off the sweat on his forehead with the back of his hand and shook his head. He had never been too good at putting money on the side for rainy days. Well, hell, he didn't have enough even for bleak days.

He pushed on until the noise of the town fell back. Then, he sat on a rock on the side of the trail and lit a cigarette.

He was seriously thinking of quitting but realized that he couldn't do it cold turkey. He had just managed to reduce their number to almost half. He drew the smoke in his lungs and congratulated himself. It was an accomplishment after all. Right there at the top with stopping drinking.

Gabriel couldn't look at a bottle of booze without feeling queasy. He hadn't even sampled a drop since that late night or early morning, better said, when he went to bed in the company of a bottle of vodka and a dead woman.

He put out the cigarette without finishing it and shoved it in the small plastic bag he had got into the habit of carrying with him when he roamed the mountain. His conscience had reared up and shamed him the first time he had crashed a cigarette butt under his heel on one of those trails.

Gabriel turned back to the fork in the road and took the other way, which led back into town but through the scenic route.

He met only a handful of people on his way, but his sunglasses hid his misery, and his lips curved up at the right moment. He nodded his greetings, and enjoyed the feeling of being acknowledged even if he didn't know those people.

The route he had chosen brought him back, practically in the heart of the town. The scent of meat on the grill buoyed his spirits, and his nose followed it to the source.

He stepped onto a terrace stretching in the shadow of about twenty or maybe even thirty colorful umbrellas, and a grin perched on his lips. He inhaled the smoky air, and decided he had just found the best place for a late lunch.

He started toward the back of the terrace with the thought of finding a table right next to the grill, and his step became livelier, his smile wider. Suddenly, the sound of a voice put a stop to all that well-being and to his stride.

Andy was seated at a table a few feet from him, and he was talking, using his big hands and wide gestures to complete the conversation. A few of the other team members listened to him and chuckled.

Gabriel noticed Anna, seated very close to Andy, and it felt good to see her laughing and feeling like she belonged. She had never seemed so carefree, and her simple beauty shone through it. She didn't seem to need her skimpy attire anymore.

Next to her, Adria awed Dan with her auburn hair and the blue-green eyes shimmering beneath her glasses. Gabriel's gaze passed over the others, and he shook his head. He was out of that group, and for good.

Gabriel smiled sadly and turned on his heels to leave the terrace. He had barely taken a few steps when a big, wide hand fell on his shoulder. He tried to shake it off while turning around to see who was waylaying him.

His amber eyes met Andy's dark ones. They assessed each other wearily for a few moments, and then Andy said, "Come sit with us, Gabe."

Gabriel's smile broadened. It had been a while since he heard that name on Andy's lips.

"I'd love to, Andy, but I can't," he shook his head wretchedly a few moments later.

"Why not?" Andy tilted his head in puzzlement. "If you came here, it means you wanted to eat. So you can eat."

"Yes, that's why I came. But the police said that I couldn't have any contact with any of you. I'm a suspect, you know that," he pointed out.

"I'd tell you what I think the police should do but you wouldn't appreciate it. Lately, you haven't liked my poignant vocabulary too much," Andy grinned mischievously. "Anyway, no one sitting at this table thinks you're a killer. And if you really feel the need, you can let the police know that you'll be having lunch with us," Andy said in a tone more appropriate for a despot whose habit was to decide everyone's fate.

Gabriel grinned, recognizing the old Andy. He had missed that guy and had had a hard time reconciling with an Andy who treated him like yesterday's garbage.

"I'll let the police know I'll have lunch with you, and then come to the table, all right?" he asked.

"Suit yourself," Andy shrugged and returned to his friends while Gabriel shook his head, his gaze following the man's big shoulders swinging.

Andy's gait was out of the ordinary. He exaggerated his swagger as if it had been a huge sign reading '*Don't mess with me.*'

Gabriel grabbed his phone out of his pants pocket and dialed the number Magda had given him when they first spoke on Saturday. She didn't pick up so he left a succinct message, informing her that in spite of her directions he was having lunch with some of the team. He shoved his phone back into the pocket, and with a deep breath, he started striding toward the table.

He didn't know what to expect, although Andy had been affable. Gabriel also felt a little self-aware when the people at the table shifted their gazes to him. A moment later, effusive greetings welcomed him, and he shed the reluctant mantle he had wrapped around him. He joined them, and less than five minutes down the road, they talked as they used to.

"What are you drinking, man?" Dan asked when the waiter came to take their order.

"Some vodka, I suppose," Andy intervened with a big grin, looking directly at Gabriel.

"No, not for me," Gabriel shook his head. "I'll go with a coke and a fat stake," he said to the waiter.

"Come on, man," Andy interjected. "You need a drink here."

"Swore off drinking," Gabriel informed him with a shrug.

"No, really?" Adria asked, brushing her auburn hair behind the ears.

"Really," Gabriel replied with determination, and his mouth set in a hard line. "Drinking brought me only grief. I'll try my hand at being a teetotaler for a while."

"I can't believe it," Andy retorted. "You can drink a non-alcoholic beer at least."

"Not in my plans, Andy," Gabriel said, although the temptation was huge. However, he needed only to remember what he had become because of his drinking, and his will strengthened.

They lingered at the table for over three hours, in spite of the waiter's side gazes meant to make them move along. When they left the restaurant, Andy proposed that they walk Gabriel back to his B & B before returning to theirs.

Gabriel felt good. He had a hard time to keep up with everyone's questions and comments, but that wasn't a reason to complain. His grin widened when Andy stretched his arm over Anna's shoulders and pulled her to him, making her blush. He didn't miss Dan's efforts to grab Adria's fingers and his failure to cage her hand in his.

They had talked about Alex for a while. It would have been impossible not to mention the man. It had saddened them, but Andy had brought them back to the lighter side of life.

Stretching in his bed after he put out the light, Gabriel fell asleep at once, with a smile on his face. Life sometimes was good. Tomorrow might be worse, he couldn't know, but it was good right then.

CHAPTER THIRTEEN

"Are you out of your mind? A third body?"

"You know that I wasn't at fault with the first two. You know because I told you."

"And I stupidly believed you," the older man's scorching gaze burnt into the other's.

"As you should have," the reply came in a very confident tone of voice. "I told you we didn't want anything else but to roughen that girl up a bit," the guy thought to explain again.

Tension frazzled the air, and he thought to defuse it with some logical talking. As the older man started pacing and brushing his fingers through the air, the young one rolled his eyes, thinking that he needed to sweeten the pot a little more.

"She deserved it, you know it. The slut spread it for everyone but me as if she'd had the right to choose. She even had the grit to talk to me as if I were a nobody. Me! Imagine!" his voice rose with a few decibels, and a grimace deformed his features.

The other one turned his eyes at the ranting young man, baffled and falling short from understanding what the man was saying. He remembered about the rape attempts made on Mia and shook his head.

"We'd have stopped there, I've told you that. But then, that idiot came into the room, and we just reacted. After killing him *by accident*, as I've told you before, we didn't have any other choice. We had to kill the girl too. She'd have talked, man," he threw his hands into the air.

The older man looked somewhat skeptic about that explanation. Something didn't sound right. It didn't really wash out.

The woman would have talked anyway. Physical and sexual assault wasn't something that the police didn't take seriously.

Regardless, he knew he would aid the man before his eyes. That had been his duty all his life, and duty was a sacred thing for him. He had always done it, and done it well.

"All right, I understand the first two," he said hesitantly because, in fact, he didn't. At the same time, he tried to read the younger man's features. "What about this one?" he pointed to the body they had just rolled down the ravine.

"He knew about you and ran his mouth. He would have brought you a lot of grief. I had to shut him up. Just because of you," the reply came, and the younger man's eyes brimmed with adulation toward the other.

The latter shook his head at a loss of words. He didn't believe that he had the means to solve this third crime. The first two kept the police running in circles, but this one would take the lid off a huge bucket of vipers.

"What could I do?" his eyes turned back to the other.

"I have an idea, don't worry. We'll both get out of this without a scratch, you'll see," the young man nodded with assurance, and then he proceeded to explain in detail what he had in mind.

The other gaped at him during the presentation of the entire plan, shaking his head now and then, struggling with his exponentially growing astonishment.

He couldn't believe the inventiveness and slyness of the younger man, and he didn't know if he should feel proud or scared of him.

When the last line of the strategy was laid out, he sighed deeply and accepted that the plan might work so he rushed to make it happen.

That evening, a mutt stumbled over the body of a young man and started yapping like crazy, fit to raise the dead. His master, a twelve-year boy, called him without success for over fifteen minutes and then struggled down the slope to put the leash on the dog and get out of there.

Soon it would have gotten dark, and his mother didn't like it when he dawdled out at night. He could bet his newest comics that he was in for a long lecture that evening.

At the sight of the dead man, comics and parental lectures flew out of his mind. The boy promptly lost his dinner and started climbing up the hill as fast as he could, in his rush forgetting about his dog and everything.

An hour later, the police had already bagged and taken away the body and combed the area. They collected the meager evidence on site but knew it wouldn't have been enough to solve that murder.

The ID on the dead guy made the inspector in charge, Bogdan Damian, call Magda. She needed to know that one of her suspects had become a victim as well. They arranged for a meeting at the morgue when the forensic team had finished gathering the forensic evidence.

Magda recognized the victim's face although it was bashed in. George Lecca had left her with the impression of a repressed personality, easily led by someone stronger. Looking at his battered body, that impression became certitude.

"The coroner will perform the post-mortem on this guy only tomorrow," Bogdan Damian informed her. "He left for Bucharest this morning and will be back only around midnight."

"Yes, I heard something about him going to a conference or something," Magda nodded, pacing the room, immune to the harsh smells of formalin and antiseptic.

She brushed her hair behind her ears and thought of a course of action. Then, she looked up at Damian and said, "I'll get Celia and go talk to the guy's friends. I know where their B & B is. You should continue with the investigation here," she added, and then she started out of the morgue.

The interviews took up most of the night. Luckily, their subjects didn't mind the late hour, although they minded the subject of their interviews. Their biological systems worked well until two or even three in the morning.

However, around midnight Magda decided to stop the discussions and continue them in the morning.

Her brain was fuzzy already, and Celia's eyes were bloodshot. They arranged for a conference at ten a.m. and went their way.

Magda got to the station half an hour before the conference. To her surprise, both Celia and Bogdan waited for her in the entrance hall, and Titi rushed to join them from the vending machine, a coke bottle in his hand.

"What's with the welcome committee?" Magda asked with a small smile. She had the feeling that something wasn't quite right.

"Big news," Celia replied with wide gestures. "The kind you won't believe," she added, nodding sagely and stealing gazes at the others.

"Now you've made me curious. What won't I believe?" she asked, and the smile never left her lips.

"Stefan made an arrest," Bogdan answered in a dry tone of voice, lifting his brows.

"I see," Magda murmured. "Who did he arrest and for what?" she asked, slightly nauseated by the news.

"Not difficult to guess, girl," Titi intervened after gulping half the content of the coke bottle. "That boy, Gabriel Something," he waved his hand in the air above his head. "I can't remember the other name right now," he muttered, after he chased the name through the corners of his mind.

"I see," Magda murmured again, unable to move. She couldn't believe what they were saying. "Why?"

Celia and Bogdan shrugged, but Titi replied without qualms, "You can choose the reason you want. Because he felt you liked the boy. Or because he is a prick and can't refrain not showing that he's a prick. Because he heard voices last night, and those voices asked him to do it... Should I continue?" the man asked, noting that Magda was gaping at him nonplused.

She could only stare. The man spat out some very bizarre motives, and she didn't find the words to stop him.

Celia and Bogdan were trying to smother their laughter but didn't seem very successful in their endeavor. Titi was on a roll.

"All right," Magda gathered her wits when she noticed Titi's frown. "First, we go and see Gabriel Barna. We'll take it from there," she decided and started with huge strides toward the holding area.

They found out where Stefan had put Gabriel, and Magda merely marched into the room. She didn't bother knocking on the door.

Gabriel sat at a wooden table, his wrists cuffed. He was leaning his shoulders on the wall behind him, and the amber of his eyes had become liquid. A black bruise marred his chin, and his left eye told the story of a fist which had met his face with high velocity several times.

Titi looked at the man and shook his head. He was convinced that Stefan would be toast now. Magda couldn't disregard such brutality as it went against everything she was trying to build there.

Celia covered her mouth to stifle any sound. The bruised state of the man before her eyes shocked the woman to the core.

Bogdan winced noticing the signs on the man's face but didn't say a word. He pushed his hands into his pockets and leaned back on the door, waiting to see what would happen.

Through narrow slits, Magda studied Gabriel's features, and then her eyes fell on his cuffed wrists.

Stefan had turned to the door when they entered, and a victorious light glinted in his eyes.

"Would you care to tell us what we're looking at?" Magda asked with frozen calm.

Stefan shrugged and replied, "This is the man I arrested for the murder of George Lecca. He'll soon confess to the other murders as well," he assured Magda with an ugly smile widening over his lips.

"I see," she said without inflexion. "We'll see about that, won't we? I suppose you have everything you need to support your allegation."

Stefan stood up with pent-up anger. He wanted to say something, but Magda stopped him with a gesture.

"First, though, I'd like to know how he came by those injuries," she inquired in the same eerie-like tone of voice that scratched on Stefan's nerves.

"He resisted arrest," Stefan replied, throwing an ugly gaze in Gabriel's direction.

"I see," Magda murmured and turned toward Gabriel. "Did you resist arrest?" she asked him very matter-of-factly.

Gabriel sneered, dashed his eyes to Stefan and considered him with disdain. Then he replied in a distant tone of voice, "Tough to resist arrest when someone jumps on top of you while you're sleeping, inspector."

"You can't believe him. It's his word against mine," Stefan roared.

"Actually, it's evidence and witnesses that make me believe something," Magda retorted.

Stefan gaped at her, not understanding exactly what she meant.

"I suppose that if I talk to the people at the B & B, they will support your story," she said in a mild tone of voice.

"I will make sure to bring you their statements," Stefan started to the door, ready to go and gather those testimonials on the spot.

"It doesn't work that way," Magda stopped him with a hand on his chest.

"What the heck do you mean?" the man's voice shook with anger.

"I mean that Damian will go and take the statements at the B & B," she replied, making a sign with her head toward Bogdan to start cracking.

"He'll not come back with the truth," Stefan tried to push by her, but Titi stepped in front of him.

"He will, and I will trust those statements," Magda warned him in a hard voice.

"Now, take off those cuffs," she ordered Stefan.

"No, I won't. He's a murderer and you want to sweep it under the rug because..."

"Sorry," she replied with amusement. "That won't work," she advised him.

"I have proof he did it," Stefan countered her.

"That's quite interesting, I'd say," she replied pensively.

"Why?" Stefan's eyes narrowed, studying her.

"Because he's got a very strong alibi for when the crime took place," she replied pragmatically.

"Who the heck would give him an alibi?" Stefan exploded.

"If you had done your homework as we did, you'd have known," the chief inspector cut it short. "Now take those cuffs off his wrists," she ordered in a tone of voice that didn't broach disobedience.

With a sense of dread, Stefan unlocked the cuffs and pulled them off the man's wrists brutally. As Gabriel was watching Stefan's face, he noticed that the man expected a sign of weakness from him so he didn't want to give Stefan the satisfaction of hearing him groan.

Magda's gaze stopped on Gabriel's features for a few seconds, and then she turned and said, "Stefan, you have the day off today."

"What? Are you out of your mind? I told you that I have evidence..."

"Then give your evidence to the forensic team and go have fun," she answered and took her eyes off him.

"It is with the forensic team," the man growled.

"Great, then Titi can show you out, won't you?" her eyes shifted from Gabriel to the forensic expert.

The man nodded, and with a sign, he invited Stefan to follow. The inspector shook his head as if he couldn't believe what was happening and left the interrogation room in a huff.

Once the door closed behind him, Magda turned to Celia, "I want you to check all of the last victim's possible relations."

"Not a problem, boss," the young woman chirped. "Would you allow me to do a little research on something else first? Related to the case, of course. I just have a hunch," she shrugged.

"No problem, do it," Magda replied, and Celia left the room in very high spirits.

Magda gazed at Gabriel for a few seconds, and then she opened the door and waved a Probationary Inspector to come in and take a seat at the table.

She sat in the chair opposite Gabriel. She looked at him for a few minutes, and then asked, "Do you need a doctor?"

The man's gaze swept over her features, his fingers drumming absently on the scarred wooden table where sometime in the past, another jailbird with an original vision had carved some abstract anatomic parts.

Apparently, Gabriel found what he was looking for on her face because he decided to answer.

"There's no need. He roughened me up a bit. It's no big deal. I've had worse," he shrugged.

"No dizziness, nausea, blurred vision?" Magda inquired.

Gabriel's lips twitched, and he shook his head.

"I don't see two of you, if you're worried about that. I could do with a coffee though if you don't mind. I didn't have time for one this morning. I had to come here directly from my bed, as you can see," he opened his arms, pointing to his uncovered chest and the frayed gray shorts he was wearing. "I hope you don't mind that I didn't comb my hair or brushed my teeth," he jested. "I wasn't allowed to wear shoes either."

Magda closed her eyes and counted to ten in her mind so that she wouldn't start yelling.

"I apologize on behalf of the department for what happened to you, Gabriel," she folded her hands on the table.

She looked like a schoolmarm, prim and serious, despite the flimsy yellow dress, covered with small white flowers.

"We haven't had any plans to arrest you today. So that you know," she continued.

"Oh, Stefan screwed with your planning, I see. My arrest was penciled in the schedule for tomorrow?" he inquired with sarcasm in his voice.

"We know you couldn't have killed George Lecca," Magda answered. "Adrian," she turned to the other inspector. "Please, call someone to bring some coffee here. Our guest needs one, and so do I. Probably, you'd like one too."

"I'm on it," the man jumped off the chair and started punching the phone keyboard, looking for a specific number, while striding toward the door.

"You don't need to call from outside the room," Magda said. "It is not a state secret, after all," her lips pursed.

Adrian turned to her, a bit rosy in the face. Even the tip of his ears had blushed, and Magda had to stifle her laughter.

They waited for the coffee to be delivered, Gabriel looking at Magda, whose gaze was focused on something she was reading on the screen of her phone. Meanwhile, Adrian was studying Gabriel with unconcealed interest.

Once the coffee came, the interview began, despite Gabriel's inappropriate clothes or lack thereof.

CHAPTER FOURTEEN

On Friday evening, they gathered again in the conference room. Stefan was present as well, glancing from one to the other, a lot of anger in his gaze.

He hadn't been allowed to do too much since the morning of Gabriel's arrest, and that was galling him.

The man practically growled remembering how he had been sent away from the police station only to find out later that Gabriel had been freed. On top of all of that, they had even offered him excuses on behalf of the department.

He looked at the faces in the room with blatant distaste. His eyes lit with fury when they swept over Titi, who had dared to throw him out.

Everybody was waiting only for Celia, who had told Magda that she had something important to print, but she would be there in less than ten minutes.

The coroner read the newspaper, sipping his coffee, and Bogdan Damian entertained the forensic expert with a story narrated in hushed tones, so that he would be the only one to hear.

Stefan's mouth pursed realizing that everybody avoided looking at him or talking to him. Even Magda read emails on her phone, as if he hadn't been there.

Celia erupted in the room with joy on her face, waving a bunch of papers. Everyone but Stefan smiled at her, though the woman took place right next to him, placing the papers face down on the table.

"All right, let's begin," Magda turned her phone off. "Doctor..."

"As I already wrote in my report, the cause of death was strangulation, and that didn't happen at the place where the victim was found. He was killed somewhere else and dumped down that slope afterward," he said checking his file, just for show.

He knew very well his findings so he didn't use files for anything other than props. It was imposing to make a show of looking over papers.

"I know that we determined that he was carried there in the truck of a car. We have the make and year, but there are tens if not hundreds or thousands of that type of car around. Anyway, once we have a suspect, we can check the interior of the suspect's car, and that will nail it."

He stopped for a few seconds and sipped from his bottle of water to refresh his throat. Then, while screwing the lid to the bottle, he looked at the expecting faces of his colleagues.

However," he continued, glancing at Magda, "before getting to that, the murderer seasoned the poor victim. George Lecca's body was covered with bruises on his torso, face and back. I'd say it shows without doubt that the killer has a serious anger management issue," the doctor concluded.

"That's for sure," Titi concurred, folding his hands on the table and leaning forward. "We didn't find too much evidence at the crime scene. Actually, as the doctor said, the crime scene should be somewhere else, and where that place is, we haven't found out yet," he waved his arms ruefully.

"We will, don't you worry," Magda replied quietly. "We still have a few cards up our sleeves," she smiled with assurance, and Stefan winced inwardly.

The woman's self-confidence didn't spell anything good for him. He wanted her to fail. It was a visceral need.

"Anyway, we collected only one piece of helpful evidence," the forensic expert continued, and Stefan smiled with satisfaction as he knew what the man was talking about. "We found a piece of a t-shirt, if you remember. The victim's fingers curled around it. As someone had already worn it, we could have obtained DNA and everything from it," Titi mentioned.

"Do you mean to say that you haven't bothered to get the DNA yet?" Stefan jumped up of his seat and roared. "Are you all stupid or what? We could have had the killer downstairs right now, and you're playing at what?" he thumped his fist on the table, and Celia flinched.

"Sit down," Magda said quietly.

Stefan refused to heed her order, but Lucian Cassian's gaze compelled him to listen. He plopped back on his chair, shaking his head with disbelief.

"My God, I'm working with a bunch of idiots," he muttered. "I'll go directly to the Superintendent with that. Just wait and see," he leaned forward and wiggled his finger under Magda's nose.

The woman looked at him with indifference for a couple of seconds, and then she said, "Maybe you'd better listen to the rest first, and then, you can plan your appointment with the superintendent."

Her voice filled Stefan with dread. He didn't understand why she wasn't scared and didn't ask for a reprieve. She should have been. That investigation had been flawed from day one, and she was the cause.

"Titi," Magda signaled the forensic expert to continue.

The man cleared his throat, shook his head, looking at Stefan, and only then, he went on with his presentation.

"We haven't analyzed the t-shirt because it would have been a waste of time and money. Listen, boy," he stopped Stefan when this one opened his mouth to interrupt again. "That piece of cloth comes from the tee we've had in the evidence room since the first two murders. You brought it in, for God's sake. Now, I checked the cameras," he mentioned, full of satisfaction to notice the beads of sweat on Stefan's forehead. "What do you think we saw on the tapes?" he asked in a waggish voice.

Stefan swallowed hard and avoided the man's gaze. His heart pumped anxiously. Something was very wrong there. He didn't know what but he was caught in the middle.

"You haven't thought of that, have you?" Titi shook his head toward him. "I've told you before, and I'll tell you again. You don't have imagination. That's why you didn't get promoted, son," he gave another shake of his head.

Titi turned to Damian who leaned back in his chair and looked like he had swallowed a lemon, his face ashen and the light in his eyes dulled.

"Your face looks so pretty on the film, boy. You should have tried to become a movie star, not a policeman," he shook his head.

Damian froze and couldn't find the words to reply. His face pasty and his eyes stone hard, Stefan turned to him.

"You, prick. You nudged me to arrest that guy. You played me like a... a..."

He didn't finish what he wanted to say but launched over the table to grab the inspector's shirt. Cassian intervened and shoved him back in his seat with a push of his hand in the man's chest.

"Calm down, Stefan. It's not his fault that you don't think first and react afterward. He just took advantage of your idiocy."

Stefan dropped in his seat heavily, his breathing rugged. He wiped off the sweat on his forehead with his forearm and groaned, shaking his head. He couldn't comprehend what was going on.

Celia reached out to pat his hand but changed her mind, remembering how the man had reacted to that in the past.

"Apart from all that," Celia intervened in a soft voice, "I've found something else that's very interesting," she pointed to her papers.

Stefan turned his tired eyes toward her. Defeat was written all over his face. It didn't really matter what she had found.

"That piece of evidence gave me the idea to look. I looked first in Stefan's history. Then, I turned to you," she said looking steadily at Damian. "You have a step-brother," she continued. "His name's Alec Josan, known also as Al, among his colleagues."

"So?" Damian asked dryly.

"I remember he was very vague about his whereabouts when it came to the first two crimes. When George was killed, he hadn't been with his colleagues in town and said that he had napped that afternoon."

"So the boy slept, what's the problem?" Damian fairly yelled, panic storming through his mind. The tips of his fingers had become numb, and a powerful fist squeezed his heart. His life was just crumbling around him, and he couldn't do a thing to stop it.

"It is not so simple, Bogdan," Magda replied morosely. "Facts speak, and evidence never lies."

Damian rubbed his temples with the tip of his fingers, trying to calm the raging fury. The impulse to throttle the woman pushed at him.

He was aware that his career had ended, and his life wasn't worth a cent. Still, he preferred not to hear the sentence come from someone else's mouth.

"Your involvement in throwing the guilt upon someone else in relation with the last crime is obvious," Magda mentioned. "You didn't try to steer us in Gabriel's direction from the beginning, unless you worked on Stefan even then, but this time, you messed with evidence, Bogdan. You wouldn't have done it for just anyone, would you?"

Damian shook his head in denial, but didn't look up. He couldn't gather his thoughts to form a plan or come up with an explanation.

"We've already arrested your brother. He's downstairs. You know what's sad?" she asked, and Damian's eyes turned finally to her.

His gaze was immobile and his features cut in stone. The man knew when to throw in the towel.

"He has just tried to convince me that you killed everyone, and he didn't have any involvement. He was a bit fuzzy about your motives, but otherwise, his narration was coherent enough."

Damian's bitter chuckle filled the conference room. He shook his head again, and rubbed his eyes.

"And you believed him, of course," he said turning his gaze to her once more.

"I'm afraid not. I wouldn't believe his story even if you corroborated it," she shook her head. "The evidence doesn't point to your presence at the first crime scene. You falsified evidence for the second murder, but you are only an accessory after the fact," she pursed her lips with disappointment.

"Am I also under arrest?" he inquired in a hoarse voice.

Titi and Cassian looked at him as if he had lost his frigging mind. His question wasn't even worth an answer.

However, Magda just nodded and signaled Celia to read Damian his rights and arrest him. Then, she turned to Stefan.

"I'm afraid you'll have to answer for that abusive arrest, Stefan. Next week, there will be an investigation. I thought you should know about it," she gathered her things and left the room without looking back. She carried too much weight on her shoulders right then and didn't need to add Stefan's feelings to that.

Stefan watched everyone leave, and then leaned back in his chair, closed his eyes, crossed his arms over his chest and shook his head.

"It's time I left this job. Something with security would work better for me," he pursed his lips and nodded.

CHAPTER FIFTEEN

Gabriel left his things in the room he had taken at the B & B where he had stayed before and which he had liked. He went out to spend some time on the patio, and then, he decided to wander around for a while.

He had returned to the town at the foot of the mountain on the first train, and now, after a good breakfast, as good as he remembered, his feet itched to move.

He crossed the road toward the edge of the forest and started walking up the trail. He needed to get to the glade he had found during his trips around the town the last time he had been there and where he had planned the rest of his life.

It seemed just fitting to go back there. It was point zero in his journey.

His memories of that town were somewhat bitter. He hoped to make better ones. He believed that he could do it if he wanted it enough.

The man breathed deeply and welcomed the cool bite of the autumn air in his throat. He had left the town in summer, and he had loved it then. Now, in September, he fell in love with the town and the mountains all over again. The rustle of leaves and the way the light of the sun fleeted through the branches of the trees brought him a measure of peace.

After spending an hour sitting on the grass in the glade, thinking, making more plans and just wasting time, Gabriel started back down the trail. He didn't hurry. He still had time to take the next step in his big plans.

Less than fifteen minutes later, he reached the outskirts of the town and the corner surrounded by trees where the B & B blended in the landscape. He had only fifty more steps to get to the front door or the inn when he froze for a couple of seconds.

Magda faced the building, fidgeting with the strap of her shoulder bag, and nibbling the side of her forefinger.

He approached her slowly, and she turned her hazel eyes to him. She studied his features for a few moments, and then a smile curved the full lips he had been dreaming about for so long.

"You got my message," he said in a raspy whisper, his eyes never leaving her oval face, framed by the dark thick hair.

He wanted to touch her, but didn't dare, although his fingers twitched. His avid stare soaked every line and shadow, and his thoughts rolled in turmoil around his wants and needs.

Magda nodded, touching his arm with shy fingers. Gabriel leaned toward her, and her eyes widened. The man grinned, wiggled his brows and then touched her lips with his. It was just a feathery brush, sweet and breezy. Still, he lingered over her bottom lip, shaping it to his heart's content.

"My God, I've been waiting for this for such a long time," he whispered against her mouth, his breath electrifying her sensitive skin. "Like a lifetime."

"Maybe a month and a half tops," she whispered back, and he chuckled, kissing her hard afterward.

"You're so precise in everything," he shook his head with amusement. "We should make an interesting pair, sweetheart," he brushed his fingers of the side of her face, awed that he was given the chance to touch her.

"Will we make a pair?" she wondered, trying to read his deep-set eyes.

"That's what I hope," he replied. "I'm moving here so we might as well give it a try," he shrugged.

"Your romance is killing me," Magda replied dryly, and Gabriel chuckled again.

"You're out of luck there, if you're looking for romance. With me, what you see is what you get," he pulled back pointing his fingers to his chest.

"Well, I can't say I don't like what I see," she lifted an eyebrow, analyzing the man's physique in a way she hadn't dared before.

"Enough to have dinner with me?" he asked, moving in and brushing his lips of her mouth once more. He loved her taste. Hell, he craved it, and he couldn't have enough of it.

"Dinner's good," Magda whispered, brushing her fingers on his back. "We can start with dinner."

Gabriel shrugged and gave her a lopsided grin. "We do have to start somewhere. Although, I would have thought that we started some time ago," he searched her gaze.

"You're not wrong," she put her hand on his chest, and lifting her face to him she nibbled at his throat, making him chuckle once more.

"Then, let's just continue," he clasped her fingers in his hand and brought them to his lips.

Then, he turned her hand over, and his tongue flicked over the sensitive skin in the middle of her palm. Feeling her shiver, he stopped, kissed her briefly and pulled her with him.

"They serve excellent dinner at a restaurant nearby. Let's try it. We'll talk some more then," Gabriel explained, his long stride eating the ground and making Magda shake her head.

"I love your plan, Gabriel. However, I'd like it even more if you matched your stride to mine. I don't want to trot along," she pulled at his arm. "I'm not a horse, you know," she chided him.

Gabriel slowed down, and leaning over her, he kissed the top of her head.

"All right, sweetheart. I'll leave the speed to you. We'll move as fast or as slow as you want. We have all the time in the world," he said, and he meant it.

Sliding his arm around her shoulders, he showed her the way, his pace less hurried than before. He had what he needed. Now, he needed to stop running and enjoy it.

EXCERPT FROM THE NOVEL A SUITABLE EPITAPH

PROLOGUE – AXEL'S VISION

The woman had been flirting with him for over fifteen minutes before he invited her to accompany him in the garden for some fresh air. Glancing out the patio doors into the darkness, she smiled. That was exactly what she'd been aiming for and she consented freely to follow him outside.

After all he was a very well built man. Maybe quite too well, she thought when she noticed him for the first time. Her mouth watered while her eyes perused the expanse of his broad shoulders and strong hands.

She needed a man. It had been some time since a man's strong hands aroused her. Probably, too long, if she considered the flutter in her belly.

The physical desire had been compelling enough, but the signs hinting to his wealth had been more important and decisive for her. The man was wealthy enough for her tastes. His suit wasn't a cheap imitation but a true Armani. She'd always had an eye for such things.

They strolled leisurely along the gravel path as she clung to his sturdy arm. He murmured some inconsequential things and she didn't bother to listen.

The power she could feel under her fingers was as exciting as the heavy smell of the roses lining the one side of the trail. She smelled romance in the air and smiled.

A few more steps and the roses made way to berry bushes. The smells changed and the heat of the summer night enveloped them in a humid cocoon.

The shingle path disappeared and she stumbled when her foot stepped on cracked soil. Both chuckled although embarrassment powdered her cheeks with a slight blush. He silently provided more support to her and a giddy feeling bubbled in her veins.

When he hastened his steps, she giggled softly and commented playfully on his haste. He was watching the trees, distracted, and didn't give any sign that he'd heard.

That determined her to bring a halt to their fast advancement through the garden. It might have been romantic, yet it didn't seem very wise. She was alone with a man she'd just met and didn't know anything about him.

It was her first time there and she hadn't been aware that the garden grounds were so extensive and secluded. Besides, while she had all intentions to flirt with him, she didn't have any intentions to succumb to his charms that night.

It was never a good idea to give in too soon. She wanted much more than a tumble in the hay and that meant that she had to play hard to get for a while. Men liked the hunt. They enjoyed the scent of their prey and the efforts that came with their chase.

The huge man glanced at her. His eyes showed understanding and he allowed her to move at a slower pace. She was wearing stilettoes and her feet thanked him. When she put on her high heels that evening before the party, she hadn't meant to wear them on that hard ground.

Once they were about forty meters away from the house and in the shadow of the trees lining that side of the garden, the man grabbed her arm and nudged her to a deserted corner. He put enough strength behind his action and the brutal move startled her.

A shiver played on the back of her neck and sent tentacles along her spine and the back of her legs. A spine-chilling feeling replaced her light-hearted mood from before, but she didn't take it lying down.

She tried to reason with him at first. She preferred to assume that maybe he was too anxious to be alone with her and that was why his attitude changed. Her well-chosen words fell on deaf ears though, and she stopped pretending. She began to oppose him but it was as if she'd been trying to stop a river flow.

Indifferent to her pleas, he dragged her for a few more meters. She continued pleading with him because she didn't see any other solution, but her attempts failed. She replenished her efforts to fight him and tried to dig her heels in the ground, but the soil was too dry and she couldn't get any traction. She just stirred a cloud of dust that rushed to find a home in her pores.

Her legs turned to jelly and she barely kept herself upright. Something was definitely wrong with what was going on there. Both her self-confidence and sense of safety had slowly skulked away during the forced walk through the trees.

Tinges of electrical shocks ran through her arms. She panicked and tears burnt her cheeks. She felt ashamed of her weakness and tried to hold them back, but the cold fingers of fear kept squeezing her heart in an iron fist, and her breath became ragged.

Probably sick of her puny attempts to detangle herself from him, he finally stopped and moved to stand before her. Through the stream of her stubborn tears she surveyed the man's stony face with dread. The man wasn't even blinking and that disconcerted her more. He was just staring at her with dead eyes which quashed her hopes.

She tried to say something again, but now she didn't find the strength to push the sounds past her lips. Her throat refused to work and her mouth was drier than the soil she felt under the thin soles of her fancy shoes.

She glanced back to the house with renewed albeit premature expectation but the trees hid it from sight. Her lips quaked when she realized that no one could see or hear her.

A corner of the man's mouth lifted in a satisfied smirk, and that sneer was a splash of cold water over her face. Even though her anxiety was climbing and reaching new heights, she understood that what he felt for her was nothing else but contempt.

That came like a shock. Not the first that evening to be sure, but this one packed the power of a live wire and her mind scattered looking for an explanation.

She'd always been certain that men admired and even worshipped her. She'd basked in their burning glances often enough and she knew that she didn't delude herself.

She stared back at him with tired eyes. She tried to decipher what lay there behind the mask but her intuition had taken cover somewhere and didn't offer any help.

The sturdy man studied her for a few moments and then, he reached out and fisted his hand over her silk blouse. His touch brought her back to the reality which had twisted a pretend romance into a horror movie. Fear bubbled near the surface now and, as her brain scrambled the signals, she was about to burst into a hysterical laughter.

In that frozen moment, that soft blouse which caressed the curve of her breasts became the most important thing in her world. She was very proud of that top as it was one of the symbols she attached to the life she'd built for herself. She'd turned that expensive piece of silk into a tangible proof that she'd exceeded both her and other people's expectations but, more important, that she'd escaped her birth circumstances, which had confined her to the working class.

The sight of that dark and threatening hand on her precious top brought a glimmer of dread but also made her see red before her eyes.

The beefy hand jerked hard and the flimsy blouse fell apart rendered to rags. Her dismay and the pressure of her fury at the sight of her prized chemise ruined ruthlessly pushed a warlike cry past her quivering lips.

She abandoned any rational thought and jumped the man. Her shoes found soft spots in his shins and made him grunt. Her nails targeted the handsome and ruthless face she'd admired just minutes before and left blood in their wake.

He fought her back. The slap of his backhand unbalanced her. She stumbled back and cried out again and not only because of the pain. This cry echoed the terror that had swiftly crept into her bones and fried all her neuronal cells. The man was strong and she didn't have the ability to defend herself against that brutal show of force.

Her cry died soon, though. Another man grabbed her throat from behind and his fingers gripped her as a vise and smothered the sound.

She questioned and berated herself. In the heat of the fight she'd failed to hear the other man's steps. Still, she promised herself to go down swinging.

She tried to claw into his skin but he didn't show that he registered any kind of pain. Running on instinct only, she directed her stilettoes to his shins but she couldn't say for sure if she succeeded. His fingers burrowed harder into the delicate skin and left bruises behind that marred the flawless whiteness of her epidermis. Her air pipe constricted and the woman slid slowly into unconsciousness.

Before she blacked out, she had just enough time to feel other fingers knotted in her hair. She was beyond terror and anxiety. Her impotence overwhelmed the solitary corner of her mind that was still functioning. The last thought that passed her mind was that she couldn't buy or fight her way out of that. She'd lost the game and that was her night.

The slight flicker of life in her body just made it interesting for the men around. The third man who'd grabbed her hair, threw her on the hard ground in the shadow of a bush pregnant with red drops. Her skirt climbed up and the whiteness of the exposed skin of her legs lit the darkness.

The three of them were still looming over her. They stared at her fallen body for a few seconds.

One of the attackers smirked with satisfaction, his eyes going from her body to the red berries. The ugliness in his sneer showed that he knew that the beauty of the red fruit went hand in hand with their poison and he found it befitting the situation. The woman was about to get what she deserved. Poison deserved poison.

Axel woke up with a jerk and his half-lidded eyes surveyed the bedroom. The light of the moon reflected in the glass panels of the south wall and filled the room with shadows in the corners.

His heart pounded in his chest. For one brief but agonizing moment, he'd feared that he was there with those men, who were still staring at the woman's body, which was lying in the shadow of that bush.

Now, wide awake, he breathed deeply and closed his eyes in relief. He was still in his house.

Axel's relief was short lived. He'd scarcely closed his eyes, that he had another vision of the woman's broken body.

She was lying down on that hard and dry ground which he'd seen in his dream. Now, a monotonous rain whipped her mercilessly and washed the pattern in blood which had been painted on her body, feeding it to the dehydrated soil.

The vision was so in-depth that Axel could even see the rain drops clinging to the woman's eyelashes. The light in her eyes had dimmed at first and then vanished. The lines on her forehead had deepened and marked her passing years on her face.

A few hours earlier, that face had been flawless. Now it was marred with an x high on her left cheekbone and her features showed weariness, pain and despair.

Axel flexed his fingers and wiped his damp palms off on his thighs. Axel's visions weren't always so detailed, but there were exceptions, such as the one that he'd had that night.

When the image finally blurred, Axel exhaled in a whoosh and then breathed in deeply. He wiped his forehead and noticed that his fingers weren't as steady as he knew them.

Axel shook his head and got off his bed and tried to stand. He had to lean on the night table for a few seconds before trying his wobbly legs again.

In the usual course of events, the man wouldn't have needed help to find his bearings. Axel knew his lair as well as the back of his hand and could find his way through the rooms even if he hadn't pulled the curtains aside to have the room bathed in the light of the moon. Still, that night, he needed the support of the walls to reach the bathroom.

There, he leaned on the lavabo and stared at his reflection in the mirror. Staring didn't help though. He turned on the tap and filled his fists with cold water which he liberally splashed over his face.

When the trepidation had left his body, Axel drank a mouthful. His mouth had been dry and his tongue was almost stuck to the roof of the mouth.

It wasn't enough. He brushed his teeth and only then he left the bathroom. He started towards his terrace but hesitated. He was restive and needed something more than to just listen to the owls in the night and the sounds of the lake.

With a shrug, he turned around and left his bedroom. He needed a glass of his best whiskey to wash away the metallic taste of death which still lingered in his mouth. His toothpaste hadn't succeeded in chasing it away. He also needed to make a decision.

Axel didn't know the people in his dream, but he knew the house. He'd seen that garden before. He'd strolled around it many times in the past and knew exactly where to find that pregnant bush.

Now, he had to decide what to say to the police and how. He didn't want to reveal how he knew about the crime but they would ask and he needed to plot a strategy.

EXCERPT FROM THE NOVEL
AN IMMIGRANT

The echo of hasty steps coming from the direction of the Gigue reached his ears. With trepidation, Victor lifted his head and stared unblinkingly into the night.

Anxiety and fear nudged at him and he pushed hard with his palms into the ground to move. Pain instantly radiated everywhere in his back, but resolute, gritting his teeth, he tried to crawl under a tree. It felt as if he had moved through molasses. Each inch he covered brought more sweat and aches.

'At least I'm alive,' Victor thought. 'But not for long, if I don't move out of this darn trail,' he groused and pushed harder, gritting his teeth to contain his grunts.

"He fell somewhere here," a strong male voice shredded the silence.

"Are you sure? I can't see anyone," a throaty female voice replied with evident doubt.

Victor stopped any movement and tried to become one with the ground. He knew he was in the shadow and they couldn't see him.

"I can hear him," the woman said with enthusiasm, and Victor grimaced.

'How the heck can you hear me?' he wondered and his eyes widened. His fingers dug into the floor of the grove, as if he wanted to anchor himself.

'I'm not saying jack,' he thought. 'I'm not so out of my mind that I'm talking without being aware of that, aren't I?'

"Yeah, I hear him too," the man's voice replied. "He's kept his humor so he mustn't be in a very bad shape," he noticed drily.

Victor's eyebrows shot up his forehead. 'Who the heck are these people? More important, what the heck do they want with me?'

"I don't hear anyone around," the woman said. "Take out your flashlight," she ordered.

'She's like a drill sergeant,' Victor mused, listening intently to every sound they made.

VICTOR GAVE UP ANY pretense when the light swept over him. He didn't know those people but there were only two options —either they came to save him or finish him. There wasn't any way around that.

He lifted his head, and gnashing his teeth, he turned to the light. The flashlight blinded him, and this time, he couldn't hold a groan.

"He's there," the man said, and rushed to kneel next to Victor. "Hey, buddy, are you still with us?" he asked, and Victor sensed the smile in his voice.

Victor grunted and nodded once. He didn't know whether he still had his voice. His eyes searched the man's face. Satisfied he had never seen him before, he laid his head on his folded arms again, and closed his eyes.

"Is he still alive?" the woman's voice asked.

"Yes, he is. What should we do now?" the man inquired, rousing Victor's curiosity.

'Why would he ask for her advice?' he thought, and the next moment, the man's laughter filled the air.

"Because she's the boss now," the man replied with good humor.

His words shocked Victor, and he just froze, his eyes zeroed in on Axel. He couldn't even blink.

"Now look what you've done, Axel," the woman chided her companion. "You scared him."

"He'll survive," Axel answered matter-of-factly, and Victor had the distinct impression that the man shrugged with nonchalance.

"Who are you people?" Victor croaked, unable to keep his mouth shut one second more.

He felt as if he had fallen in a strange dimension. This time, he was sure he hadn't voiced his question.

The woman's cold hand brushed his hair off his forehead, soothing his increasing fever.

"I'm Leah MacKay, a detective, and this is my boyfriend, Axel Arnett," she replied in a kind voice. "I'm going to call an ambulance for you," she continued.

She tried to stand up but the man's fingers closed over her wrist with surprising strength.

"No police," he groused.

He bit his lips. The sudden move had sparked arrows of pain along his spine and lower body.

Arnett burst into a hearty laughter. The sound gritted on Victor's nerves. If he had had the strength, he would have knocked the man down.

"Sorry, pal, the police are already here," Axel explained with cheer, making Victor lock his teeth again.

Leah pried his fingers off her wrist gently and took her cell phone out of her pocket. She dialed 911 and explained to the operator who she was and that she needed an ambulance and her team at the Sarabande.

Defeated, Victor sighed and laid his head on his arms again. He'd seen a commercial once with a small hedgehog coming out of a hole just to be hammered down once more. Now, he was the hedgehog. He had lost control of his life. 'Eh, it's not for the first time,' he mused.

Axel Arnett leaned over him and whispered, "Everything will be well, don't worry. She's the best."

"That's what I'm afraid of," Victor grumbled, prompting Axel to chuckle.

Axel liked the man and felt satisfaction that they got to him in time. Hopefully, he would survive.

Axel felt the strength in him and counted on his built. He wasn't a man that could be easily taken down.

BOOKS BY ROXANA NASTASE

Mayhem on Nightingale Street – McNamara Series – Book One

Scents and Shadows – McNamara Series – Book Two

McNamara Series – Box Set (Book One – Mayhem on Nightingale Street & Scents and Shadows)

A Suitable Epitaph – MacKay - Canadian Detectives Series - Book One

An Immigrant – MacKay - Canadian Detectives Series – Book Two

MacKay - Canadian Detectives Series – Book Set (A Suitable Epitaph & An Immigrant)

A Churchgoing Woman

Relative Bonds – McNamara Series – Book Three

Payback Is a Bitch

The Man in the Elevator

FORMCOMING:

A Change of Heart – MacKay - Canadian Detectives Series – Book Three

Did you love *Team Building with a Twist*? Then you should read *A Churchgoing Woman*[1] by Roxana Nastase!

Greed, envy and ego in a small town in western Oklahoma.

Lorna was mean and petty and wanted to control everyone. That signed her death warrant.

Discover life in a small town. Secrets, affairs and shocking surprises. If you love mysteries than you will adore this nail biting thriller.

Read more at roxananastase.weebly.com.

---

1. https://books2read.com/u/bMrDYV

2. https://books2read.com/u/bMrDYV

About the Author

Roxana Nastase has been teaching English for over seventeen years, ranging in level from kindergarten to college. She specializes in English Grammar and has had several books issued throughout the years. Her books were used with much success in schools in Eastern Europe for teaching English as a second language.

Read more at roxananastase.weebly.com.

About the Publisher

It is based in Toronto and brings to public various books: poems, novels, short-stories, children's books, language study books and non-fiction. It publishes the literary review: Scarlet Leaf Review: www.scarletleafreview.com

Our mission is to help emerging authors and poets to make their works known to the public.

Contact email address: scarletleafpublishinghouse@gmail.com